Rose
Red

JB THOMAS

First published in Far North Queensland, 2023 by Bowerbird Publishing

ISBN 978-0-6457433-0-2 (print)
ISBN 978-0-6457433-1-9 (ebook)

Rose Red
JB Thomas

Edited by: Crystal Leonardi, Bowerbird Publishing
Cover Concept & Design by: Dion Marc & Crystal Leonardi
Interior Design by: Crystal Leonardi, Bowerbird Publishing

Distributed by Bowerbird Publishing
Available in National Library of Australia

Crystal Leonardi, Bowerbird Publishing
Julatten, Queensland, Australia
www.crystalleonardi.com

This book is dedicated to Hnossa.

CONTENTS

Rose Red

CHAPTER 1

Kevin Rose lounged by an open window in his homeroom, relishing the gentle caress of a refreshing breeze that playfully tousled his luscious, curly golden locks. Despite the sweltering and oppressive afternoon heat, he found solace in this moment of respite from the hustle and bustle around him.

This day held significance for Kevin, marking the end of his senior year -- an occasion marred predictably by the malfunctioning air-conditioning system. A recurring misfortune that had afflicted him not only this year but also in the preceding ones. Rather than paying for an upgrade, the school, driven by their frugal resolve to bolster their sports programs, resorted to patching up the dilapidated unit with tape and bubble gum.

An electric buzz of anticipation filled the atmosphere as the clock ticked closer to 2:55, signalling the arrival of summer vacation, poised to free them all for a glorious stretch of 90 sun-drenched days. He was filled with an overwhelming sense of exhilaration. No longer would he be shackled to outdated textbooks and long hours of tedious homework. However, his eagerly anticipated first semester at university was scheduled to begin in August. Hooray for that, right? Not!

"Kevin!" The voice of his best friend, Sara, echoed through the chaotic classroom.

Kevin's sea-green eyes flickered open, drawn to the sight of her navigating through the crowd of students, their voices melding into a symphony of noise.

"Hey there!" Kevin beamed, reaching out to brush his fingers through the stunning cascade of hair reminiscent of a sunset over red rocks. "Are you as excited as I am? Never again will you have to step a Gucci hoof in these halls."

"Oh, this place hasn't been half bad," she teased, lightly swatting his shapely hand away from her vibrant, fiery crimson locks. "You know, these are truly the golden years of our lives."

"Can't relate," he deadpanned, his voice laced with a touch of dry humour.

A playful glimmer danced in her eyes as she locked her gaze with him, her deep amber contact lenses concealing her natural brown eyes. Sara was known for her ever-changing eye colour, and sometimes she even showed up at school with mismatched hues.

"You're going to look back on this place fondly," she insisted, a tinge of nostalgia colouring her words. With a graceful motion, she tucked a stray strand of hair behind her ear.

He shook his head, a wry smile playing on his lips as he carefully packed his belongings into his well-worn leather satchel. "Nope. I'm not going to miss a thing."

"You're right," she chuckled softly, the mirth lacing her words. "Fuck this place."

Kevin nodded in agreement. High school held little to no fond memories for him to dwell on. Enduring four years of social hell at Blue Grotto High had left a mark on him. Moreover, this was the last day he would ever have to see Tyler Glace. The mere thought of the tall, blond, broad-shouldered baseball player sent shivers down Kevin's spine. Tyler was an embodiment of physical male allure, scorching with a heat that could rival Satan's nut sack.

He fervently beseeched the heavens, pouring his heart and soul into every prayer, yearning for Tyler to suffer an endless stream of defeats on the baseball field. He hoped with every fibre of his being that Tyler would face the harsh chorus of boos echoing through the school or seek refuge in another school blessed with a better team. However, it became clear that his entreaties reached a god who appeared either impervious to his pleas, incapable of hearing, devoid of understanding, or simply non-existent.

Deaf, dumb, detached, or dead. He had embarked on a spiritual journey to implore the divine presence of the Goddess of Mercy and Compassion, seeking her guidance in the art of bestowing mercy and compassion upon those who refused to extend it to him. This meditation posed a considerable challenge as he attempted to envision himself gracefully turning the other cheek, yet somehow found himself inadvertently wielding a pink dildo carved from solid rose quartz and swinging it at the athlete's head.

"Hello?" Sara asked, poking Kevin on the tip of his nose with her scarlet fingernail. "Where did you go just now?"

"I think I am seriously beginning to suffer from heterophobia," he grumbled.

"You're such an idiot," she snorted, pushing at him. "Why don't you jump Tyler's ass? It's the last day of school. You've achieved your grades. You even got your one point away from a perfect score on the SAT. Any college will snatch you up. What can this place possibly do to you now? You do know there is no such thing as a permanent record before eighteen, right? They make that crap up to control us. If you look these teacher's directly in their eyes, you can see the fear shivering back."

Kevin arched a meticulously groomed eyebrow, a shade of gold. The astute observation made by his best friend struck a chord within him. Perhaps, in fact, he could find an unexpected thrill in committing his first transgression. The resonating chime of the school bell filled the air.

"Ah, crap! Look at the time!" She jumped to her feet. "It looks like you get to keep your goody-goody record forever, Pretty Boy."

Kevin's eyes rolled in exasperation, finding solace in the fact that Tyler had managed to keep his mouth shut throughout the day. However, in an unexpected turn, a tantalising aroma of mandarin and lime wafted towards him, causing his senses to stir. That accursed cologne, an intoxicating blend that always made his body tense and his breath deepen involuntarily. From that moment on, the mere whiff of that fragrance would forever leave him glancing over his shoulder, consumed by an unsettling sense of unease.

"Are you relieved, Queer?" A resonant voice, tinged with a hint of annoyance, asked from behind.

He lowered his head, releasing a weary sigh while shaking it, his frustration reaching the breaking point. And there he stood, Tyler Glace, the reigning monarch of the Blue Grotto High baseball team, known as the undisputed King Jock. It seemed nothing could ever run its course smoothly, not even on the last day of school.

Without a moment's hesitation, Kevin swiftly pivoted, unleashing a lightning-fast strike fuelled by the entirety of his body weight. His clenched fist found its mark, connecting with a precise blow to the side of Tyler's left eye. Caught completely off guard, the jock faltered, his steps stumbling. Taking full advantage of the opportunity, Kevin lunged towards the towering figure, propelling him backward into an unfortunate collision with a nearby desk. The force sent them both sprawling to the ground in a cacophony of tangled limbs, echoing with a resounding crash.

"Sweet Jesus hanging on the cross!" Sara cried, jumping back from the flailing arms, kicking legs and tumbling chairs. "Go for the eyes, Kev! Go for those baby blues!"

Kevin disregarded her and the clamour emanating from Mrs Brown, reaching a tipping point. His limit had been breached. No longer was he willing to put up with the verbal bullying. The moment had arrived to assert himself, signalling to everyone that he would no longer passively dismiss their actions with a frosty silence.

He wailed on the stunned jock.

"Hey!" Mrs Brown shouted, struggling to make her way through the crowd of excited onlookers. "Break it up this instant! I mean it! Oh my god! Kevin, stop trying to rip out Tyler's hair! I said stop!"

"Oh, shit!" Sara howled. "You're about to be a bald-headed bastard, Ty! Kev's going to scalp your ass! Show him why you wear a feather in your hair, Kevin!"

CHAPTER 2

"I can't believe you!" Kevin's mother seethed, her voice dripping with disbelief and frustration, as she maneuvered through the sluggish traffic. Her gaze darted towards him, her eyes harbouring a mix of concern and apprehension, as if she saw a malevolent force taking root within him, slowly blossoming into a venomous and wicked entity. "What possessed you to get in a fight on your last day?"

"I apologize for Mrs Applebee interrupting your root canal," he said, tenderly nursing his swollen bottom lip, a painful reminder of the blow Tyler had delivered. Anger surged within him, fuelled by the audacity of that jerk to strike his face. The world around him turned tunnel-visioned, consumed by a kaleidoscope of righteous fury the moment that elbow had made contact. "But I finally gave him exactly what he deserved."

"What did he do?" she inquired, executing a sharp left turn onto Mollusc Avenue.

Kevin shrugged, his slender shoulders rising and falling dismissively. "I'd rather not discuss it."

"You left him with a bruised eye and attempted to tear out a large section of his hair," she reminded him, skilfully swerving to avoid colliding with Mr Yukimura on his bicycle, who was blissfully unaware of the commotion. "You even resorted to biting him. What could he have possibly said to provoke such a violent reaction?"

Gouging Tyler's eyes out had been Kevin's initial instinct, thwarted only by the intervention of the vice principal, who had pulled him away before he could position his thumbs.

"He said something he shouldn't have," he replied, rolling down the car window to let in a gust of cool air, hoping it would quell his simmering rage. "And I gave him exactly what he's been yearning for all these years—a reaction."

"I'm astounded that you would misuse your karate skills like this," she shook her head, her disappointment palpable.

"I didn't use Tae-Kwon-Do," he calmly corrected her, seething with frustration as the memory of his training momentarily escaped his enraged mind. In that moment, he tapped into his primal instincts, unleashing a flurry of furious strikes, combining the force of his fists, teeth, nails, and powerful kicks. His offense was relentless, leaving a bewildered Tyler with no choice but to defend himself. "I used Pissed-Off-Homo on him."

"Hey!" She snapped, reaching over to lightly slap him across the back of his head. "I don't approve of those ugly words coming out of your mouth, young man. You're better than that!"

"Sorry," he muttered, rubbing where she had struck him.

"You should be," she told him with a slight smirk. "You're far too pretty to speak and behave this way."

He rolled his eyes.

"He called you the F word again, didn't he?" She asked, turning onto Merman Street.

"Q word this time!" He snarled, puffing up like a sour faced bull-frog. "Why did I have to be born different?"

"There is nothing wrong with being different," she gave him a soft smile.

"I'm attracted to guys, Mom," he sighed, cheeks burning a pink-ish gold just talking to her about these things. "How can something not be wired wrong in my brain?"

"Society is changing, Kevin," she told him, pulling into their driveway. "You're only being yourself. Your true, authentic self. That's no crime."

He peered pensively out of his window, captivated by the scene before him as his mother parked. His gaze fixated upon their elegant grey stone house, accentuated by the striking ice blue shutters that adorned its windows. Standing proudly at two stories tall, it stood as the lone dwelling in the neighbourhood that lacked a garage, a testament to its age and antiquity, having been erected long before the others had come into existence. Even if his mother had any desire to change this, the limited space available rendered it void.

The house itself exuded an undeniable charm. Boasting four generously proportioned bedrooms, three luxuriant full baths, a large kitchen, a dining room infused with a comforting ambience, an expansive sitting room, and an enchanting outdoor garden complete with a pool, it was a haven of comfort and security.

With a gentle cajoling tone, his mother's voice beckoned him from his reverie, accompanied by the sound of her opening door. "Come on," she entreated, a note of warmth lacing her words. "Shall we grill our would you prefer ordering takeout?"

He decided on grill.

CHAPTER 3

Tyler burst into his bedroom, a storm of emotions bubbling within him. With a resounding thud, he forcefully slammed the door shut, the decisive click of the lock sealing him off from the outside world. Overwhelmed, he inhaled shakily, his unsteady breath a testament to the turmoil consuming him.

Across the room, he marched with purpose, his steps echoing his inner unrest. The bathroom door swung shut with a resounding bang, echoing his frustration, before being locked tightly, shutting out the world once more. Leaning back against the door, he fought valiantly to hold back the tears threatening to escape, the battle within him plain to see.

His trembling hands outstretched before him, a visible manifestation of his anger and humiliation. Yet, beneath the seething rage, a profound sadness tugged at his heartstrings. Weary but determined, he moved towards the sink, his gaze fixated upon the reflection staring back at him from the oval mirror.

Bloodshot and brimming with unshed tears, his blue eyes bore the weight of his emotions, each unspoken struggle etched into their depths. A darkening bruise marred his left eye, a vivid reminder of the altercation that had taken place. Dismissing his baseball cap with a toss, he delved deeper into his own shaken reflection, seeking solace within his own troubled gaze.

Placing his trembling hands on the cool edges of the marble sink, he sought stability amidst the chaos, taking in measured breaths that steadied his racing heart.

Homo! Queer! Faggot!

Kevin's emerald eyes had fought a battle to conceal their hurt, yet Tyler, even in that fleeting moment, discerned their distress. Those eyes bore the scars of pain, echoing a deep sorrow. Within their depths resided an overwhelming sense of betrayal, suffusing every fibre of his being.

As Kevin lifted his gaze, his eyes fixated intently upon Tyler's countenance. The handsome visage bore the traces of a battle fought within, a testament to the emotional strife he had weathered.

"Homo!"

His bottom lip trembled.

"Queer!"

His fingers tightened on the sink edges.

"Faggot!"

A single tear escaped his injured eye, tracing a delicate path down his cheek, followed by another tear from his right eye. He sniffled and gazed at the silver bracelet adorning his wrist.

Gently, he massaged his shoulder, still able to sense the lingering ache from where the fair-haired youth had sunk his teeth. Though the fabric of his shirt had shielded him from a break in the skin, something profound had transpired in that moment of violent contact. It should have jolted him to his core, yet instead, it served as a poignant reminder of the constant struggle he waged against himself, pushing his emotions deep into the recesses and locking them away in darkness.

All the hidden sentiments he had diligently bound in the silent abyss now shattered their bonds, unfurling like a torrent from the depths of his being. His carefully constructed barrier around his true nature, his sexuality, crumbled before the luminous green eyes of Kevin, who patiently awaited the revelation of his authentic self.

Oh, God!

I'm a horrible person.

Fuck.

CHAPTER 4

Kevin savoured the flavour of his jerk chicken paired with fragrant coconut rice. With his plate now empty, he carried it to the dishwasher, wishing his mother goodnight before going to his bedroom. He had to get up early in the morning for his parttime gig at his favourite shop: Tarot Moon, the local new age bookstore.

Within the welcoming walls of Tarot Moon, Kevin found solace—a sanctuary that resonated deeply within his soul. The store's owner, a long-time family friend of his parents, had created a space where Kevin felt truly understood. It was here that he sought refuge during his journey of self-discovery, perusing an eclectic collection of books that helped him navigate the complexities of his awakening sexuality. The internet had also played a pivotal role in his quest for understanding, providing valuable resources and support. In this regard, Kevin counted himself fortunate, blessed with a loving and understanding mother. Her profession as a dentist attuned her to subtleties, and when he had come out to her as gay, it had felt almost redundant—no straight man had such perfect teeth.

He ascended the stairs to his room, his gaze briefly catching the photo of his mother's great-great grandmother, proudly taken during her time on a reservation in Oklahoma.

"Show him why you wear a feather in your hair, Kev!"

He shook his head. Desert Flower Penelope. Each time her name drifted into his memory, it triggered a vivid symphony of pistol shots reverberating through the air, accompanied by the resonant voice of a woman on horseback proclaiming, "The gold is for the people!" It was complete fiction. She had married a doctor.

Settling into his comfortable computer chair, Kevin's gaze settled upon the cherished photo of his late father, ensconced within an exquisite sterling silver frame. His father, an incredibly handsome man, had met an untimely end at the age of 38, his life tragically cut short by a heart attack.

With a tender touch, he traced the delicate silver vines adorning his cherished photo, evoking a deep sense of love and nostalgia. The memory of that horrible day lingered vividly in his mind, even though he had only been ten years old at the time. They had both been in their garden, basking in the warmth of companionship and playfulness. As he tossed the ball to his dad, anticipation filled the air, but in an instant, everything changed.

Caught in the enchantment of sunlight filtering through the swaying willow branches, he was momentarily blinded, forcing him to squint and regain his sight. His heart skipped a beat as he beheld his father, face down in the grass. Questions formed on the tip of his tongue, eager to understand what had transpired. Yet, the radiant beams of sunlight dancing before him obscured his vision, and he struggled to comprehend the sudden absence of his father's presence.

Fear gripped his heart, an overwhelming sensation that surged through his entire being. In the blink of an eye, his father, once his playful companion, had vanished from his side. It felt as though his father's very soul had chosen that precise moment to depart, ascending on a brilliant stream of sunlight, leaving him alone and bewildered.

Shaking off the weight of those memories, he sought distraction in the digital realm, signing into his Instagram.

RoseRed: *Hello? Are you there, Michael?*

He lingered, his gaze fixated on the messenger box, patiently anticipating a response. The guy had a knack for savouring every passing second. Suddenly, a melodious chime resonated, instantly capturing his attention, signalling the arrival of Michael's reply.

VermillionWings: *Hey, Kevin! I just woke up. Got a long night ahead of me.*

With a sly smile, Kevin tapped his fingers across the keys. Michael was a true creature of the night. As his iTunes sprung to life, emanating the nostalgic charm of FM-84's 80's synth melodies, Kevin effortlessly shifted his attention back to his message box, ready to resume his cyber dance with the other guy.

RoseRed: *What are you going to do?*

He reclined in his comfortable chair, luxuriously extending his socked feet onto the sleek surface of his desk, cradling the keyboard in his lap.

VermillionWings: *I was thinking about heading out and catching a bite to eat. I need to get a few pieces completed for a client who needs them for her showing.*

Kevin nodded knowingly, finding the topic of food a comfortable conversation. It was a guaranteed haven, where potential pitfalls were few, unless, of course, someone happened to be a fervent advocate of veganism. Not that he harboured any animosity towards vegans— Sara embraced the lifestyle without imposing her beliefs or incessantly seeking offense at every turn. The last thing Kevin desired was to emotionally burden anyone, like a captor holding someone hostage, by unleashing a tirade about the challenges of being the only gay in the village.

RoseRed: *I just finished eating jerk chicken with coconut rice. My mom learned how to cook it from my dad. He made some great dishes back when he was still with us.*

VermillionWings: *I like my meat rare, and I have never liked rice. It reminds me too much of maggots. Can't stand the stuff. Creeps me out.*

Kevin smiled to himself. To each their own.

VermillionWings: *Have you seen the remake of Fright Night yet?*

Kevin's response reverberated with a resounding "NO." Having already laid eyes on the trailer, he couldn't help but feel underwhelmed. As a devout fan of the original 80's flick, his expectations were sky-high. It had etched a place in his heart, gifting him laughter and sheer delight. The dance sequence at the club had been nothing short of awe-inspiring, while the seductive scene in front of the crackling fireplace had exuded a mesmerizing sensuality.

When it came to remakes, Kevin often found himself disinterested. The elusive search for a truly exceptional remake had proved fruitless. He preferred originality.

RoseRed: *No. I have not seen it. I've read mixed reviews. I love the original. What did you think about it?*

VermillionWings: *I don't have an opinion yet because I've not seen it. Would you like to see it with me?*

Kevin's heart skipped a beat as he teetered on the brink of toppling over from his chair, nearly defying gravity. Could this be real? Was he, in fact, being invited on a date?

RoseRed: *I don't even know you. I don't even know what you look like. You've never even shown me a picture.*

Rose Red

Why did his heart surge like a bullet train racing through Shibuya? His excitement soared, accompanied by a vibrant buzz pulsating within his chest, while butterflies danced and darted in a whimsical frenzy along the lining of his stomach.

VermillionWings: *We have spoken like this for the past month. I'm not a big fan of cameras. They never seem to capture me. I don't take them because I'm a very private person and my work is very popular. You've seen my website and all the insane reviews. If everyone knew what I looked like, I'd never get any peace when I do go out anywhere.*

Kevin cocked his head to the side.

RoseRed: *How do I know you're not some psycho? You could be a crazy serial killer who uses the blood of your victims in your art?*

The reply was almost spontaneous.

VermillionWings: *I've not seen a picture of you either, Kev. How do I know you're not some serial killer? We're both taking a risk here.*

Kevin blinked. A hint of disappointment etched his face, accentuated by a slight pursing of his lips, betraying a subtle wince in response to his own forgetfulness. Meanwhile, his throbbing lip served as a constant reminder of the intensity of his emotions. He decided to change the tone.

RoseRed: *I guess you could say I instigated a physical assault at school today and got my bottom lip split. I'm really upset about it. My lovely kissable lips. Woe is me. Woe I say! Woe!*

He found himself drawn to Michael, enticed by an intriguing allure. There was an indescribable quality to the way Michael typed, a hypnotic rhythm that captivated his attention. Yet, he wondered if he was reading too deeply into the subtle nuances of their interaction.

It was just black letters being typed across a white screen. He had nothing else to go on. Why was he being drawn in like this?

VermillionWings: *What happened to instigate this physical assault, Mr Change the Subject So Fast I Had to Do a Doubletake?*

Kevin laughed at that.

RoseRed: *He called me a queer and the raging homosexual came out in a glitter explosion. I can only assume by the shocked looks I received that my head spun around like the Wheel of Fortune because I only really remember being dragged from the room kicking and screaming about how I was going to wear his eyeballs as earrings or something like that. It's all a blur really. I'm sure it will be all over TikTok and a billion memes generated.*

If so, I should demand royalties from each view and share.

It had felt so good when his fist had connected with the side of Tyler's face. Four years of pent-up rage exploding to the surface like lava in a split second. Oh, it had been glorious!

VermillionWings: *Wow! Sounds like this jerk had it coming then.*

Kevin nodded, realising Michael could not see him agreeing with his words.

RoseRed: *It's over now. I never have to worry about it again. Graduation is Thursday night and I never have to see him again. Hopefully he won't even show up.*

He experienced a sense of relief, as if a weight had been lifted off his shoulders all because he had finally stood up for himself. Simultaneously, a pang of guilt crept in, silently reproaching him for descending to such an ugly state. The expressions of disappointment on the faces of his teachers and principal had left an indelible impression on him, making him feel a little remorseful.

After all, he was a Gemini, known for their multifaceted nature. When they go low, I go to Hell.

VermillionWings: *Mr Senior is finally entering the real world. It's nothing like what the movies make it out to be. There's going to be real stress beyond those school doors. Bills, bills, and more bills. So much responsibility. Anyway. Congrats on that! How about this then? Why don't we meet up at Joe's Pizza on Friday night at 8?*

Kevin tapped his keyboard with his thumbs. Uncle Joe's Pizza was a popular place, so there would be lots of people. It sounded safe enough.

RoseRed: *That sounds like a plan.*

What the hell? Was he really going to do this?
Yes. Yes, he was. It was time to take chances.
He was gay. It was time to meet other homosexuals.

VermillionWings: *If we hit it off, can we go for a moonlit walk on the beach as well?*

He was going to have Sara call his cell every hour on the hour, and if he didn't answer she was to call the police immediately.

RoseRed: *I'm down.*

He couldn't believe it. The realization dawned upon him that he was going on a date with a nineteen-year-old, who thrived as an online art designer, with a thriving business of his own. This was going to be his first gay date.

Having ventured onto Michael's website, he found himself

utterly mesmerized by the sheer magnitude of his talent. He possessed an unparalleled ability to transcribe anything onto a canvas, leaving many critics astounded. It became evident why college education had never crossed Michael's mind, for he had taken the bold step of establishing his own enterprise at a mere sixteen years of age, amassing countless raving reviews from delighted patrons. His creative masterpieces commanded prices ranging from five hundred to several thousand dollars, attesting to his skills.

VermillionWings: *I'll see you at 8. Look for the tall, dark, and extremely handsome danger...I mean stranger.*

Kevin laughed out loud. He hoped it was true. Not the danger part. What the hell had he gotten himself into?

RoseRed: *Excited. Look for the blond sun worshipper with a busted lip.*

He hit ENTER and waited for a reply.

VermillionWings: *It's a date! See you soon, Kevin.*

He smiled and logged off. He quickly snatched up his phone and started sending a text to Sara.

Kev: *OMG! You are not going to guess what just happened!*

Sara: *You reached the prostate.*

CHAPTER 5

Michael reclined in the luxurious high-backed office chair, relishing the comfort it provided as he took a moment to appreciate the mesmerizing glow emanating from the computer screen. The room, enveloped in darkness, amplified the aura of solitude that surrounded him. In this modern era of boundless technological advancements, he marvelled at how effortlessly everything seemed to fall into place—a world where desires were readily quenched at the flick of a switch.

Suddenly, a faint sound disrupted his reverie, diverting his immediate attention. His captive's lapse in remaining quiet proved to be a grave misstep.

Swiftly, he swivelled his head towards the source of the noise. "Excuse me, but I find myself parched. Might I trouble you for a drink?"

The young man bound to the high post bed could only whimper in his gag and struggle as the dark headed being rose with fluid grace from the desk, letting the chair twirl in a slow lazy circle. His shadow seemed to be a living entity all its own and it only made the darkness that much deeper. Those terrible fingers began to grow long and longer and just as sharp as the glistening wet fangs descending from his pink gums.

He loomed over the terrified guy like a night terror stepping into the waking world, shattering a safe reality. Michael pulled him in close and sunk his teeth into that tender throat.

The smell of sweat and fear filled his nostrils and he moaned, paying no mind to the man struggling in his vice-like embrace. He bit down harder and deeper, taking in every bit of the human's vital essence.

After a few moments he pulled back and licked his fangs, realising the guy was staring blankly up at him.

"Oh, well," he said flatly, lifting the corpse by the throat and throwing it from the bed. It hit the dark hardwood floor with a heavy thud and rolled once, lying flat on its back, face facing away from him.

His eyes filled the darkness with a crimson malevolence. "You wouldn't have made a good vampire anyway. There was no spark in you."

CHAPTER 6

Kevin lounged behind the elegant counter at Tarot Moon, engrossed in the latest edition of Velvet Moth. The enchanting melodies of "Music from the Pleiades" filled the air, emanating from the surrounding speakers. As he flicked through the glossy pages, his eyes fixated on a stunning model showcasing a pair of leather boots he yearned to wear. Imagining himself donning those boots, he envisioned an enhanced stature, but also the inherent danger of a potential fall that could break his neck.

Amidst the ethereal atmosphere, Mrs Davenport's voice interjected, her words laced with wisdom and a touch of playfulness, as she arranged shimmering quartz on a wooden shelf beside the mystical smoking fountain. "Keep dreaming, Baby," she remarked, her voice carrying a comforting tone. "With your radiant golden complexion, you're destined for a different kind of allure."

Kevin couldn't help but chuckle at Mrs Davenport's observation. Indeed, his sun-kissed tan rendered him ill-suited to emulate the flawless efforts of those vampire enthusiasts who revelled in the gothic realm. The unfairness of it all struck a chord within him, punctuating his wistful longing for a different aesthetic.

"I know," he affirmed with a nod, delicately turning the page, his gaze captivated by an array of exquisite masquerade masks. Crafted from the finest materials including supple leather, precious gemstones, and ethereal feathers, they emanated an undeniable glamour. Each mask was a testament to artistic craftsmanship, resonating with sheer beauty.

"I find myself longing to wear these things though," he mused wistfully. "I wish I had the time to make myself this flawless. Perhaps I could embrace Bubble Goth."

A subtle smirk played upon his lips as his eyes caught sight of an enticing advertisement showcasing meticulously custom-made vampire fangs, designed to fit flawlessly within one's mouth. The creator of these masterpieces, undoubtedly possessing the skills of a dentist, appeared to have found a prosperous side venture. Contemplating the possibilities, he pondered discussing the matter with his mother—a connoisseur of inflicting pain upon the masses—during those rare moments when boredom overcame her.

"You would do well to pay heed to your appearance," Mrs Davenport interjected, gracefully approaching to inspect the object of his fascination. "Especially if you want to capture this hot guy you've been talking with online."

He immediately felt himself blushing.

"How do you know about that?" He asked, looking around with spooked eyes, making sure nobody was eavesdropping on their conversation.

She tapped her third eye. "A little birdy told me."

He was going to have to poison that little birdy's seed. Sara never could keep a secret from the resident witch.

"Well?" She asked, smiling with those painted red lips. Her teeth were white, and the bottom row was slightly crooked in the front. "What does this Michael look like? Sticky beaks want to know."

"Tall, dark, and dreamy," he answered her.

He didn't know what the guy looked like. He had never seen a picture of him.

"So that means you have no idea what he looks like," she stated matter of fact, placing both bejewelled hands on her wide hips.

He looked into her dark eyes. They were heavily painted with black eyeliner and mascara. He had never seen lashes so long before. They couldn't be her real ones.

"I do so!" He lied, scratching the tip of his nose." If you had internet, I'd show you."

She flipped over a few Lenormand fortune cards on the counter and pursed her lips.

"You can be anybody you want to be on the Internet, Kevin."

He got a cold chill. It went howling down his spine like a hungry wolf.

"Do you think I should give this a shot?" He asked, watching as she flipped over three more cards. "We're supposed to meet at Uncle Joe's Pizza."

He hopped off his stool and walked around the corner to where she was looking at them. He gazed down at the colourful array of cards, asking her what she was getting from them.

Her eyes were aglow when she looked at him. "They speak to me of adventure in moonlight and a love you won't be expecting. Danger, secrets, and discovery."

"Oh, is that all?" He asked, turning to walk towards the door. "I'm going to go home now and lock myself away in my tower. I'll focus on college for the next four years."

"Get your butt back here," she laughed, playfully snatching hold of his arm. "You survived high school. I think you can survive your first blind date."

He gave her that Crest white smile. "I'm going to have Sara call me every hour to make sure I'm still breathing."

She nodded her head in a sage manner. "That is wise, young butterfly. Does Mommy Dearest with the tooth-drill know?"

He bit his bottom lip and looked away.

"What?" She asked, cocking a pencil thin brow.

He refused to meet her gaze.

"What?" She asked again.

He took a deep breath in and looked right at her. "She gave me a bag of condoms for him. She didn't know what size, so it is an array of sizes and colours. Some even glow."

He watched her put a jewelled hand to her mouth and gasp in horror.

"I'm offended she thinks he's the top." He mumbled.

Mrs Davenport snorted and then howled with laughter.

The silver bell above the shop door jingled. It looked as though Mrs Long was in for her weekly reading. The poor thing was terrified of what tomorrow always had to bring.

"Good afternoon, Mrs Long," he waved, giving her his brightest smile.

She replied by giving him a weak one in return. It looked as if she had been reading one too many omens again. She was going to scare herself to death if she wasn't careful. He began to wonder how her heart was.

"Come along, Ella," Mrs Davenport said, taking the shorter woman by the arm. "Mind the front for me, Kev."

He nodded.

Mrs Long looked white as a sheet.

"It was a dream, Naomi," he overheard Mrs Long call Mrs Davenport by her name. "It had to be."

She was allowing Mrs Davenport to lead the way behind a thick curtain of beads to the reading room which was across from the Reiki room. The curtain rustled with small clicks and shimmering colours.

"The young man was so handsome, and he moved without using his feet. He seemed to be wearing the mist as if it were a cloak."

Kevin rolled his eyes.

Sounds like someone had been reading too much Anne Rice again.

He decided to get lost in his magazine again. The stress of trying to figure out what he was going to wear was killing him. It was only Uncle Joe's Pizza. Should he go casual or dressed to kill? He didn't know what the rules were for first dates.

He needed help.

"Sara," he spoke, reaching her voicemail. "I need you to call me as soon as you hear this. I need help." He paused for dramatic effect. "What am I going to wear on my date?"

He put his phone down, turned the next page, and his phone began to vibrate.

It was a text message from Sara.

Sara: *A condom.*

CHAPTER 7

Graduation surpassed Kevin's expectations of what could be deemed entertaining. The gymnasium overflowed with a jubilant crowd, creating an electric atmosphere. The ceremony itself was impeccably organized, adorned with vibrant decorations and accompanied by an inspired selection of music. The pivotal moment arrived when Mrs Applebee handed him his pre-college diploma, solidifying the realization that he had finally bid farewell to Blue Grotto High for good.

As Kevin sat in the passenger seat of Sara's sleek red Mustang Convertible, he relished the refreshing caress of the cool night breeze through his hair, grateful for the jacket that shielded him from its chill. Sara fearlessly pushed the boundaries of speed, going over the limits set by law, but Kevin found himself unaffected by her audacity. Secured by his seatbelt, he wasn't going anywhere.

In this exhilarating moment, the melodious tunes of "Lost Boy" by The Midnight filled the airwaves, amplifying the sense of liberation and boundless possibilities that lay ahead.

"I am going to strangle my grandfather," Sara said, slamming the brakes at a yellow light. "I can't believe he actually yelled during prayer."

"WHERE ARE ALL THE WHORES MY GRANDDAUGHTER TALKS ABOUT?" Kevin mimicked, getting looks from a few pedestrians on the busy sidewalks. "PAPPY HAS A KNEE FOR YOU!"

She gave him the evil eye lightning quick.

"I wanted to die!" She snapped.

"Everyone was laughing," Kevin snickered, turning down the music. "Well, everyone but the whores."

"He pretends he's senile so he can get away with murder," she hissed, smacking his hand away from the radio, causing him to pout at her like a kicked puppy. "He's an old pervert and never touch a redhead's radio, bitch."

Kevin rubbed the top of his abused hand, letting his lower lip tremble just a little, causing her to snarl at him. It made him smile. She was too easy. You're not even a natural redhead. If I pulled your hair out, the roots would be black.

"Are we really going to Peter's party?" He asked, watching the light turn green, getting his head thrown back by her swift take off.

"Duh!" She said, turning onto Dolphin Circle where all the big houses were. "He's had this bash planned since the beginning of the spring semester."

Kevin nodded, crossing his arms firmly over his chest. Although he didn't typically indulge in parties, he couldn't bear the thought of Sara going alone. Moreover, an unsettling feeling of apprehension gnawed at him, knowing that Tyler might seek revenge if he showed up.

During the graduation ceremony, Tyler had shot him a peculiar glance that lingered in Kevin's mind. The black eye he had inflicted upon him seemed strangely muted, skilfully concealed with a touch of concealer to diminish its striking prominence. His mother must have been behind that bit of makeup magic.

It wasn't like he felt bad for Tyler or anything. The homophobe had had it coming for years and he finally got the reaction he wanted.

"Are you worried Ty might show up?" Sara asked, looking over at him.

He nodded his head. "You know I am. I don't want to ruin Peter's party by breaking something expensive over Tyler's head and getting Peter in trouble with his parents."

She laughed at him. "I am sure lots of things will be broken by the time this party is over. You have me with you. Let that jerk try something. I have an ice-pick under my seat."

"A lot of good that'll do," he said, wishing she would try and be serious for once. So, he began to imitate her perfectly, right down to her mannerisms. "Wait, Ty! Don't jump my gay best friend just yet. I'll be right back. Hang on, okay? Okay? Promise? Cross your heart? Good! Have any of you sluts seen my keys? Oh, damn! There they are! Does anyone know how to climb trees? Peter? Didn't your mom get you a monkey for your twelfth birthday? Oh, that's right! It ate the nanny's face and had to be put down. Dammit, Ty! I told you to wait! Get off him! Like, oh my god! Hang on, sassy gay best friend! I got you!"

"I do not talk, nor do I act like that," she said, pulling into the huge driveway where dozens of cars were already parked haphazardly over the finely manicured lawn.

Peter's magnificent home stood as a testament to his family's opulence. Just like Sara, Peter was also a rich kid. His house boasted three grand stories, exuding an air of grandeur. Notably, the premises housed not only an expansive heated indoor swimming pool but also an inviting outdoor pool.

Music wafted through the air, reaching their ears from the vicinity where they had parked. It was evident that Peter was skilfully harnessing the power of his cutting-edge speakers, amplifying the enjoyment for all.

"Do you think there will be lots of drinking?" He asked, unbuckling himself.

She sat there and just looked over him. "No. Not at all. We're good Christian kids."

"Where are his parents at?" He asked.

"I'm not sure," she answered, opening her door as he removed his black jacket, revealing his yellow tee. "I think his dad is in New York and his mom is in Cyprus. Something about offshore drilling and an upset island goddess."

"Now I know why they weren't at Graduation," he said getting out with her, looking at some people he didn't know walking across the lawn towards the large front doors. He felt bad for Peter. It must be rough. At least his mom was always here for him.

"Come on," Sara said, coming around to his side and taking him by the hand. "We're supposed to be partying like its 1999. Let's go see Peter."

"Race you to the door?"

"Are you mad?" She glared daggers at him. "I can't run in these heels."

He pursed his lips.

"GO!" She shouted, taking off, leaving him to gawk after her.

He stood, captivated as he watched her effortlessly glide across the expansive lawn, gracefully navigating the white pebbles with remarkable poise, all while donning five-inch heels.

All he could do was applaud, his hands coming together in a thunderous display of appreciation. The sight he had just witnessed was nothing short of breath-taking, leaving him amazed. Comparing himself to her athletic prowess, he struggled even to run in sneakers.

"Girl, bye!"

CHAPTER 8

Peter's party exuded a pleasant ambiance, yet Kevin couldn't shake off a hint of restlessness that tugged at him tighter than his outfit. It wasn't his scene. Although he found himself on the dance floor with Sara, their moves in sync, there was something missing tonight. Even his beloved dance routine to Kylie Minogue's timeless "Can't Get You Out of My Head" failed to ignite his usual enthusiasm. The presence of an audience consisting mostly of straight individuals he had never seen before in his life, observing him and Sara flawlessly mimicking the choreography, left him feeling strangely out of place. Surprisingly, even Pete had joined in with the synchronized dance routine.

The fact that college students had infiltrated the gathering only added to Kevin's disbelief. It was clear that certain attendees would face grave consequences if their parents discovered their involvement with the older crowd.

Throughout the night, a few older teens had been casting curious yet disdainful glances in Kevin's direction, making him feel like an awkward mannequin on display in a shop window. It was making him even more uncomfortable.

As Kevin swung his arms above his head, his gaze drifted across the crowd, and there, entering the expansive sunken room, was Tyler. People instinctively made way for him, recognizing his alpha presence.

Tyler's mother must have possessed an extraordinary talent for makeup artistry, evident in his flawless appearance.

Dressed in a pair of stylish Tommy jeans and a modest yet

striking green sleeveless tee, the tall blond effortlessly exuded an irresistible sex appeal that didn't escape Kevin's notice. He looked sexy as hell.

I should have hit him with a chair.

Tyler suddenly made direct eye contact with him just as he was swinging his arms over his head side to side to the same rhythm as Sara and Pete, twisting their bodies back and forth to the beat.

"I need some air," he shouted, twisting and dancing backwards. "Going to step out."

Sara nodded, waving him off with a big grin.

He swiftly navigated the expanse of the lengthy corridor, where couples engaged in necking, gracefully veering left into the expansive kitchen bustling with blenders producing a symphony that rivalled NASA's finest. Seizing an unopened Cherry Coke, he wasted no time as he promptly veered right, down yet another extensive, unoccupied hallway, until he reached the sliding glass doors leading to the outdoor oasis—a haven adorned with an inviting pool. The melodic strains of Florence + The Machine's "Shake it Out" resonated from the outdoor speakers, infusing the atmosphere with an enchanting aura.

With a flourish, his left hand extended above his head, he danced his way to the edge of the azure waters, casting his gaze upon the glistening glass-like surface. Placing his soda beside him, he liberally discarded his shoes and socks, rolled up his pant legs, and put his feet into the refreshing embrace of the cool water. The silver moon loomed overhead, nearly achieving its fullest radiance.

The fragrant tendrils of night-blooming jasmine teasingly caressed his senses, eliciting a heartfelt smile. This delicate bloom had held a special place in his father's heart. Fond memories flooded his mind, reminiscing on the times his father diligently nurtured and harvested them, adorning their house and his bedroom with sweet smelling sprigs placed in crystal vases. As he went through day to day, an occasional waft of jasmine would embrace his senses, serving as a poignant reminder that his father's presence remained ever watchful, an enduring guardian. It was a safe and comforting scent, like the damask roses his mother grew around the swimming pool. Sweetness surrounded by thorns.

He opened his drink and took a sip as he turned his gaze up at the pale jewel. The moon was beautiful. He imagined what it would be like to walk along the cold distant shores of the Sea of Clouds, gazing at the blue earth from a completely different perspective. It would be a fantastic experience and very alien. These were the kinds of thoughts that kept him awake at night.

"Hey," a deep growl greeted him from behind, causing him to glance over his shoulder.

Tyler!?!

An immediate sense of dread struck him hard, and he fought to keep alarm from registering on his face. He took a slow deep breath in and kept his expression neutral. Did he follow me? At least the jock was alone, but that didn't make him any less threatening.

"Hey," he greeted as if nothing was wrong, and everything was right in the world.

There was no hint of surprise or malice in his tone. It was a perfectly pleasant greeting.

"Do you mind if I sit down and have a smoke away from the crowd?" Tyler asked, looking a little nervous himself.

Why does he look nervous? I should be the one nervous. And why did he greet me? He never greets me. He could have just plunged me right in the pool with a sneak attack from behind.

He cocked his head to the side. "I didn't know you smoked."

"I don't," Tyler told him, revealing a joint.

Kevin gracefully signalled his approval with a subtle gesture of his right hand, while delicately indulging in another sip of his soda to quench his parched throat. His primary concern was preserving the smoothness of his voice, as the very thought of speaking with a scratchy tone was utterly a no-no right now.

With unwavering attention, he observed the athletic individual nonchalantly discarding his pristine white Abercrombie & Fitch slides and proceeding to approach the pool's perimeter. Engaging in a masculine display, the jock rolled up his jeans before assuming a seated position, submerging his big feet into the blue embrace of the cool water.

"My parents would kill me if they caught me with this," Tyler grinned from where he sat. "Dad being a doctor and Mom a nurse. The lectures they often give."

"Just say no." They both said at the same time.

Tyler smirked and Kevin pursed his lips.

The smaller blond watched the jock light up and take a long puff, blowing the greyish blue smoke out through his nose like he was a dragon, being careful to have the smoke blow downwind. How courteous. The athlete raised his large feet out of the water, playfully wiggling his toes. "You certainly know how to pack a punch," Tyler remarked, a tinge of respect in his voice. "And you bit me."

Kevin pursed his lips and averted his gaze. He couldn't help but feel a pang of disappointment in himself for his recent actions. He prided himself for his impeccable composure and detached demeanour, he had effortlessly brushed off Tyler's remarks for an extended period, as if they possessed no gravity at all.

"I guess I had it coming," Tyler said. "Huh?"

Kevin nodded his head. "I'm not proud of my behaviour. I've never even been in a physical altercation before. You're my first."

"I know," Tyler laughed, flicking some ash. "We did go to the same school."

That surprised Kevin. He'd expected Tyler to be pissed for being mildly humiliated by a gay guy.

"You blacked my eye like a man," Tyler said, touching his injury, taking off his baseball cap. "And then you tried to rip my hair out like most girls do on television."

"You have shiny hair," Kevin deadpanned. "It caught my

attention."

He didn't mind having his fighting style compared to a girl's technique. He had watched girls battle it out at school every day. They were far more brutal than the guys. Girls stalked their victims for hours, greeting them with disarming smiles, strolling right up with a friendly wave and then clawing each other's faces off before ramming unsuspecting heads into lockers when their prey wasn't looking.

He decided to take it as a complement, even if it hadn't been intended as such. Tyler stubbed his joint out on a shiny blue tile and leaned back on his elbows. He was looking up at the dark velvet sky. Kevin was beginning to feel nervous.

What did the jock want? Why was he even out here? Shouldn't he be inside drinking and grinding up on some girl. He knew there was lots of empty rooms to screw around in.

"You hate me." Tyler said.

It wasn't a question. He had made a statement. Kevin kept his mouth closed. He didn't want to say anything at all until he was certain that was all Tyler wanted to say to him.

A few more seconds passed. He glanced over to find the jock gazing at him with inquiring eyes. He suddenly noticed just how blue they were. They reminded him of robin eggs.

"I have feelings like anyone else, Tyler," he said, making direct eye contact with the handsome jerk. He damned him for being attractive. Nobody so mean should be so gorgeous. They should be as ugly and putrid as their hearts are.

"And in that moment, I felt like I had taken all the abuse I was able to."

Tyler nodded his head, turning his face away from him, gazing back up at the large moon slowly rising higher.

"Do you hate me?" Tyler asked.

Kevin kept his eyes on the bigger blond, trying to figure out what was happening here. This was the most he and Tyler had ever spoken since their freshman year, let alone being alone together without something horrible being voiced.

"The me before our fight would say yes without even having to think about it," he answered him, pulling his feet from the water. "But hating you would be a waste of time and energy I don't have right now. So, no. I don't hate you."

Did he really mean the words that just came from his mouth? He didn't know. Perhaps he really was the better person, or he didn't want to have to protect himself from a possible physical altercation.

"I would hate me," Tyler said. The look was evident on his tan face.

"Why are you saying all this to me?" Kevin finally had to ask him up front. "Why do you care if I hate you?"

Tyler raised his muscular arm and Kevin could see a silver bracelet around his thick wrist. It read WWJD in gold script. What Would Jesus Do?

Kevin nodded his head.

"You probably won't believe me and that's okay," Tyler said. "But I am really sorry for calling you all those names."

Kevin blinked.

Huh?

"I took a really hard look at myself in the mirror after our fight, Kevin," he said, leaning forward, gazing down at his reflection in the water.

"I looked right at myself in the mirror and called myself a queer. I said it over and over and over to my reflection. Queer. Faggot. The more I yelled at myself, the more it hurt. It hurt and it really pissed me off that it hurt."

Kevin looked away from him. Was he being serious? He couldn't tell. Was this some kind of cruel trick to get him back in some way? Was there a group of his buddies hiding out somewhere, waiting to jump him the moment he allowed his guard to go down? Maybe it was time he excused himself and hurried back inside. He could then find a random door to lock himself behind and call Sara.

"I'm sorry," Tyler said once more. "It hurt me. And I know it hurt you. I'm really sorry and I won't ever do it again."

Kevin felt a little pang of remorse for him and slowly nodded his head. The jock did sound like he was being sincere.

Tyler closed his eyes. "I find it fitting it took a punch to my eye to make me see I wasn't being very Christian."

"It's okay," Kevin said, touching his own sore lip. "It's in the past now. It's two days old."

Tyler pulled his feet from the water. "I'm thirsty. Do you want me to get you something else to drink?"

Kevin stared at him. Are you serious? Did he really think he would trust him to get him something to drink? He could easily slip something into it and then take him out somewhere and beat him senseless. Okay, Mr Glace. I'll trust you. Let's just see if Jesus really is in your heart.

"If you don't mind," he answered the jock. "I could really go for a bottle of mineral water."

Tyler nodded his head, rising to his feet with ease.

"I'll be right back then."

Kevin watched him saunter away. Those jeans were tight on his muscular legs. He had thick calves and a light dusting of blond hair stopping at his ankles. All that running and lifting. He was perfectly proportioned. Too many jocks ran around with thick guns and stick legs. And that butt… Kevin shook his head. GET A GRIP! Don't mind if I do. Oh. My. God. Shut. UP! He took in a deep breath.

If the cap seal on the bottle was unbroken, he would know he could trust him. He would also make sure to look for a needle stick as well. I watch way too many crime documentaries.

He decided to move so he could see if the jock came back with anybody with baseball bats, ready for a good gay bash. That would be all he needed. The sound of bare feet padding over tiles had him glancing over his shoulder before he could. Tyler was making his way back. Alone. The bronze athlete tossed him the bottle of water, taking a seat much closer to him now.

Kevin took quick note how the bottlecap had not been fiddled with. He hadn't been serious about the needle stick. He doubted the jock was smart enough to even think of such a thing. So, he had been sincere. How…sweet…

"Tell me something," Kevin said, twisting off the bottlecap, taking a small sip as not to appear rude. He twisted the cap back on out of habit. "Aren't you concerned someone might see you sitting out here with the only out and proud gay in the village?"

Tyler shook his head. "They know I'm out here."

Kevin blinked. What the hell? Tyler pointed over his broad shoulder with his long index finger. Kevin looked. People were staring out the windows at the two of them. The three girls and two guys who were looking noticed they were being observed and quickly shut the curtains.

"Why?" Kevin asked.

"Graduation" Tyler responded. He took a sip of his soda and put the can between his dreamy legs. "I don't have to care what people think of me now. I never should have. Plus, I have a full scholarship to Mainland."

Well, shit! That's where I was thinking of accepting.

"I'm not just a jock," Tyler told him. "It doesn't matter if people know about me now, but I graduated with a 3.9 GPA." He winked at Kevin. "Not just good looking."

Know what about you now? The fact you're smart? Kevin blinked and looked at his bottle of water. He was starting to regret not checking for that needlestick now.

He struggled to keep a myriad of expressions from dancing across his face, but he was sure his nostrils flared. His GPA was a 3.8.

Tyler had a higher score than him? Inconceivable! He now had the urge to attack the jock all over again. Just hold him under the water until he stopped kicking those long legs.

He looked back to see sets of eyes peeking through the same set of curtains again. Oh, this is just stupid! He waved and they were quickly drawn shut once more.

"Okay," Kevin said, rising to his feet, making his way over to the tree where the night-blooming jasmine was hanging from. "What do you want, Tyler?" He turned back to face him.

The jock looked at him and then quickly turned his head. Was Tyler Glace blushing? Kevin blinked. OH MY GOD!

"Well," Tyler whispered, looking around. His cheeks were rosy. "When you were on top of me…and you were hitting me…well, it… your bite turned me on."

Kevin dropped his water bottle. It rolled across the ground and into the pool with a plop. His jaw metaphorically hit the cement hard enough to crack what he assumed was imported Moroccan tile.

"Don't freak out!" Tyler quickly said, holding his big hands up in concern. "I'm not going to jump you and have my way with you or anything like that. I'm a bully and I say mean things but I'm not a monster."

The scent of jasmine got stronger. It was true. Tyler was a bully. He did say mean things. But Tyler had never put his hands on him. He had been the one to put his hands on Tyler first. And even then, Tyler had never hit him. Not on purpose. Just his elbow by accident.

"I would never put my hands on you," Tyler said, looking at him with those blue eyes. "You're smaller than me."

Kevin struggled not to let his cheeks burn, but Tyler wasn't lying. He sounded sincere. This is so weird.

"Here," Tyler said, shoving a hand into his pocket and pulling out what appeared to be a napkin. The jock held it out for him to take.

Kevin slowly walked over, looked down at what was being

offered him, and quickly snatched it before backing away. The jock snorted as the smaller blond looked it over.

"You remind me of a cat."

Kevin ignored his comparison. He unfolded the napkin, seeing what he assumed was a phone number written in green marker.

He glared at Tyler. "What's this?"

"I…uh…wow. This is harder than asking a girl," Tyler shook his head, while laughing nervously. "Just call me if you want to hang out sometime. I don't care when you call or text. I'll make myself free…for you."

Kevin looked at him, then back down at the phone number, back up at the jock, then back down at the phone number written in green marker again. This was all too weird. Just what the hell was happening?

Tyler sniffed the air. "What are you wearing? It smells good."

"That's not me," Kevin shook his head, pointing up. "It's the jasmine in this tree."

Tyler's eyes followed where he was pointing. "What jasmine?"

"What do you mean?" Kevin asked, turning to where the vines were and gawked. They were gone. The flowering jasmine was nowhere to be seen. It was just a tree in a large pot. "Where did all the blossoms go?"

"Are you trying to spook me?" Tyler asked. "I once thought I saw a ghost when I was eight."

Kevin shook his head. "It was right here." He pointed and looked back at Tyler.

The jock removed his shirt and slipped into the pool. His body was nice and hard in all the right places. All that work at the gym.

"Want to join?" Tyler asked.

"I need to go find…something," Kevin lied, looking back at the tree, feeling bewildered as he turned back to the athlete.

"Do you want help?" Tyler asked, looking up at him from the water. "You're a little pale."

"No, but thank you," Kevin told him as he casually picked up his shoes and started to walk towards the patio door.

What the hell is going on? Where the hell did that jasmine go? He knew he'd seen it. It had been right there in front of him. He'd even gone up close to smell it. He had even touched the pale petals. Hadn't he? He couldn't remember.

"I mean what I said, Kevin," Tyler called after him. "Give me a call. I'll find ways to make up for every harsh thing I said to you."

He waved over his shoulder with the napkin, making his way back inside, noticing how a few certain people were looking at him with wide eyes. He looked right at them, and they quickly acted like they were busy doing everything else except watching him. Irritating. He walked around, quickly realising he had no idea where the bathroom was. It was only his hundredth time ever being in this huge house. He probably looked like an idiot walking around in a daze.

"Excuse me," he said, politely poking a guy on the shoulder. "Do you know where the bathroom is?"

The short guy turned to him, looked up at him with deep hazel eyes. He lifted an arm, pointing to the door across the room. There was a sign on it in big bold letters.

DESIGNATED BATHROOM.
DON'T YOU DARE MAKE A MESS.
I WILL FIND YOU AND I WILL KILL YOU.

"Ah!" Kevin smiled, thanking the twenty-year-old who was probably twelve.

He knocked on the door, received no reply, and stepped inside. He turned on the light. It was a very nice bathroom. He locked the door behind him with an audible click.

The floor was a lavender marble, the walls were an off white, and all the fixtures were done in silver chrome. The marble tub was massive. He loved how the toilet was even in its own separate room with a door.

He looked at himself in the oval mirror over the sink. Tyler was right. He did look a little pale. He had just seen the ghost of a jasmine vine hanging in a tree which was no longer there. It had either been a figment of his imagination, he had been daydreaming, or someone was playing one hell of an amazing trick on him, and Tyler had just told him their fight at school had given him a boner. He had turned the jock on.

He turned on the tap and splashed his face with cold water. It felt good after being out in the muggy night air with a half-naked guy. He glanced around for a towel to use, not trusting the one hanging on the silver rod next to the sink. He bent down and opened the door under the sink and found a mound of them.

He patted his face dry and looked at his reflection and jumped back like a startled cat. The fine downy hairs on the back of his neck stood up. There was someone in the mirror and it scared him. It was looking right at him. It was himself, but it was not himself. His eyes were a vibrant shade of violet and his skin looked as if it were lit up from within. And that smile. Jesus! That smile!

He carefully reached out his hand to touch the image gazing back at him with a grin on its face that would scare Death. The mirror began to vibrate. Deep down he knew. If he touched the glass, it would shatter.

His fingers were only an inch away from that violet eyed mirror image when a sudden knock came at the door. It made him jump with a yelp and the terrible beauty in the glass was gone. He was left staring into his own startled green eyes. He ignored the knocking and the rat-tling of the doorknob. He shook his head and rubbed his eyes.

He went to open the door and the metal handle broke right off in his hand with a bit of wood still attached. He stood there, looking down at his hand. Peter's parents clearly cut corners to afford all that marble and tile. He dropped the broken handle and pulled the door open, ignoring the drunk guy pushing past him, and started on his quest to find Sara. He would probably find her wasted and scaring the tourists.

He walked by a window, seeing Tyler swimming laps around the pool. Others had joined him. There was no way he was going back out there. He had his date with Michael to think about tomorrow night. But! Was Tyler serious? He felt for the folded napkin he'd stuck in his pocket. It wasn't there. His hands went deep down into both pockets. Nothing. IT WAS GONE! He looked this way and that. He must have lost it somewhere along the way. He searched his back pockets, breathing a sigh of relief his cell phone was still there.

Okay, he said to himself. I'm not going to make a scene, but I am going to make damn sure. Let's see how he reacts to me when there are others around. Here is your chance to really prove yourself Tyler Glace.

He slowly strolled out to the pool like he was the lady of the manor and made his way to stand at the edge of the water. 'Night Swim' by Owl Eyes was playing. Several people turned their heads to look at him and quickly grew quiet. This sudden silence of held breaths caused Tyler to turn around to see what caused the swift change in atmosphere.

The jock cocked a brow. Kevin placed a hand on his hip and motioned with a graceful flourish of his wrist for him to swim over. Tyler swam up to where Kevin was and stood to his full height, which brought him eye level to Kevin's knees. Water dripped down his ripped torso. Those find blond hairs catching water droplets in the light.

"Did you change your mind?" Tyler asked.

In fluid motion, Kevin squatted like a fairy on a toadstool about to pounce and looked into the jock's eyes, ignoring all the others that were on him. That's right. Stare all you want.

"It would appear that I may have mistakenly misplaced the

napkin you gave me," he spoke with a clear voice.

Tyler held out a hand. "Give me your phone."

Kevin reached into his back pocket and carefully handed it over to him. "Please don't drop it."

Tyler smirked as his thumb rapidly tapped across the screen.

"There," the jock said, handing the phone back to him.

Kevin took his phone back and rose to his full height once more, looming over the jock, letting a few more seconds of silence pass. There was so much static in the air between them, he felt like there should be a boom of thunder. Nobody else was making a sound either. All eyes were on the two of them.

"See you."

Tyler smiled. "Really?"

Kevin took a deep breath. "Depends on how my date goes to-morrow."

That smile turned into a wolfish smirk. "For my sake...I'm not going to wish you luck."

Kevin rolled his eyes and Tyler swam off.

Eyes followed him as he made his way back inside and stood in the corner. Scrolling through his contacts, he found Tyler. Tyler (the sorry jock) Glace. He sent him a quick text.

It's the rainbow classmate who scalped you. Just so you have my number. And if for some reason I should start receiving prank calls, I'll automatically assume you're the reason and set your car on fire.

What did guys like Tyler like to do besides sports and mastur-bating? He would have to do some research later.

He dismissed the spectral jasmine and the scary doppelganger in the mirror as him psyching himself out about his date and Tyler being weird. He had also broken Peter's bathroom door. He was not going to mention that bit to anyone. That could easily be blamed on some random drunk. his phone chimed. It was the sorry jock.

Tyler (the sorry jock) Glace: *I love it when you talk scary. Do it some more.*

He stood there for a moment.

Beautiful Boy: *I have no idea what straight guys even like to do for fun except chase balls, throw them, hit them, jump on them, etc.*

"SARA!" He projected his voice over Florence Welch's 'Howl' causing several people to jump and few others to spill their drinks.

Another chime.

Tyler (the sorry jock) Glace: *I'm not THAT straight. Slightly bent… for you.*

"SARA!"
Another chime.

Tyler (the sorry jock) Glace: *I didn't mean what I said earlier. I hope your date does go well. But, should it go south, text me. Also, you're a really good dancer.*

"SARA!" He roared, stalking through the crowd of very drunk dancers. "GIRL, DON'T MAKE ME HUNT YOU DOWN!" He replied.

Beautiful Boy: *Thank you.*

"Gay coming through!" He yelled, pushing his way through drunken revellers. "Move!"
And for the first time, in such a public setting, he said it with pride. The Hetero Sea parted.
"Oh my god, really?" He snapped, walking right up to his best

friend, and slapping a vibrating hot pink dildo from her hand. "Do you even know where that's been?"

She laughed, throwing her arms around him and began dancing. "In my purse! His name's Ding-Dong Betty."

I guess I'm driving then.

CHAPTER 9

Stepping into the dimly lit bedroom, Tyler found himself unable to tear his gaze away from his phone, desperately hoping for a text from Kevin. The thought crossed his mind repeatedly, pondering whether he should take the initiative and engage in a deeper conversation with the beautiful boy.

His emotions were just slightly askew, as he realized he was undeniably attracted to Kevin. Among all the guys at school, on the team, or even at that party, it was only Kevin who stirred his heart and mind in such a profound way.

Determined not to reveal the impact Kevin's mere presence had on him, Tyler resolved to get in the pool. There was no way he would allow Kevin to witness the obvious physical effects he had on him from such proximity.

His attention was abruptly caught by the illuminated screen of his computer. The rock melody of Alannah Myles "Love Is" filling the room, prompting Tyler to place his phone carefully on the edge of his sturdy oak desk. Slipping off his slides, he indulged in a moment of stretching and readjustment.

Even now, just thinking about the beautiful boy was making him...

A shrill bark came through his open window, and he quickly rushed over to look out. Gazing down from his second-floor window he saw his dog run underneath his dad's rover.

"Dylan!" He called down. "What's wrong, boy?"

The German Shepard was whimpering and growling from under the vehicle. Tyler stuck his head out of his window and gazed around. He was unable to see anything that was making his dog so upset. Did something sting him? Did something bite him? A snake?

He quickly left his bedroom, raced down the stairs, flipped on the outdoor light, and went out the front door. He padded barefoot over to the rover and got down on his knees.

"Come here, boy," he said in his playful doggy voice. "Come here. What's wrong? Did something bite you? What's the matter? Let me see."

The large dog wasn't budging. He was hunkered down and gave a low growl, teeth bared. From what Tyler could make out from the light, hair was raised along his dog's spine.

"Come here, Dylan." He reached for him with a large hand. "It's okay. I'm here. Nothing is going to hurt you."

From behind him emerged an unearthly sound, a spine-chilling noise that sent shivers down his spine and plunged him into an abyss of primal terror. As the odious stench assailed his senses, it unleashed a torrent of revulsion that churned his stomach and drenched his body in a clammy, cold sweat. A guttural growl, emanating from an enigmatic source with colossal lungs, reverberated ominously close, enveloping him in a veil of dread.

A formidable silhouette loomed above, obliterating the feeble remnants of light that struggled to pierce the darkness. Beads of perspiration trickled down his neck, while an inescapable paralysis rendered him incapable of movement or speech. Despite his desperate attempts to will his body into action, every muscle remained frozen, unresponsive to his command.

Suddenly, a scorching, razor-like grip seized his left ankle, yanking him forcefully onto his stomach with a brutal and agonizing force. His screams pierced the night, reverberating through the air as his eyes beheld an otherworldly visage that defied his human comprehension, thrusting him deeper into the depths of terror.

He screamed relentlessly, his vocal cords straining and his throat raw, unleashing a torrent of fear into the darkness. Something large, black, and quick jumped over him and whatever had hold of his ankle let go.

A thunderous roar reverberated, jolting Tyler to his very core. Dylan barked and snapped ferociously, fixated on something that Tyler's eyes struggled to comprehend. It was as if he sought to unravel the puzzle, yet each piece he connected only unveiled a more disturbing image that had him screaming louder and on the verge of losing consciousness.

"DAD!" He screamed at the top of his lungs, curling into the foetal position. "MOM!"

He couldn't breathe. His chest was so tight. He fought to move, but it was like time was super slow or he was stuck in something sticky. His heart felt like it was going to beat right through his ribcage. The sound of his blood pounding in his head was deafening him. The pain in his ankle throbbed and his vision began to get blurry.

"DAD!"

Something large and terrible loomed over him. Twin eyes burning like orange lanterns looking down through him. Those eyes told him he was nothing but meat.

He struggled and turned over, reaching out with what remaining strength he had and banged his fist as hard as he could against the rover. The alarm went off as he collapsed onto his face. Kev…

Dylan barked and howled in the flashing car lights. Everything went dark.

Chapter 10

The sound of booming thunder woke him from his deep sleep. His gaze flickered upward, meeting the sight of his ceiling. Sitting up in bed, he turned his attention to the window directly across from him. Illuminated by brilliant flashes of lightning, the surroundings danced with shadows. As his eyes adjusted to the sporadic bursts of light, he realized the power was out. The absence of its constant, subtle hum rendered the house more serene.

Stepping out of bed, he walked over to his solid oak dresser. His hand reached for a box resting atop it, anticipating the comforting ritual that awaited. With a single strike, a match ignited, casting a warm glow upon his favourite Yankee Candle: Song of Angels. Its fragrance, a heavenly blend crafted by Yankee's masterful hands, had become a rarity, now only obtainable through online auctions where bids climbed into the hundreds of dollars. His mother, the connoisseur of thrift shops, had managed to unearth a few precious treasures during her business travels. She possessed an uncanny ability to discover hidden gems in second-hand havens, earning her the title of the "op shop queen."

He stood there gazing into the candleflame as thunder boomed over his head.

Storms didn't scare him. He loved them.

Picking up his cell phone, he saw it was 3:04 in the morning. He had several text messages.

Two were from Sara and they made no sense.

Sara: *Why is cat at here?!?*

And…

Sara: *Isn't Ding Dong Betty great? Knows Betty can Ding-Dong me loves time long much so him. Bzzzz…*

He shook his head. She really shouldn't be allowed to drink. Poor thing lost her head every time the booze touched her brain.

The other text message was from Tyler. It had been sent at 1:27. It was a photo. He tapped on it. It was a picture of the bigger blonde's ankle, and it looked like something had bitten deep into him.

Beautiful Boy: *I just saw you. What the hell happened?*

He tapped SEND and instantly cringed. He'd totally forgotten what time it was. Now he was going to wake Tyler up. DING!

Tyler (the sorry jock) Glace: *My dog was barking his head off and I went outside to bring him in, and I don't know what happened after that. My parents found me in the driveway with my ankle looking like it had been caught up in a bear trap. I must have blacked out.*

Kevin climbed back into his bed and made himself comfortable. He didn't really know how to respond. He decided to start with empathy.

Beautiful Boy: *I'm glad you're okay. Did your dog attack you?*

Another photo came through and it was a picture of Tyler's ankle all bandaged up with what he assumed was a black German Shepard laying at his bare feet.

Tyler (the sorry jock) Glace: *Thanks. No! Never! Dylan would never* *hurt me. Dad found him in the backyard. He was jumping and barking at the fence, trying to get out. I was bleeding like a stuck pig and there was no blood on him. Luckily my dad is a doctor and Mom is a nurse. No need for the ER. Dad will be taking me to work with him in a few hours to get a rabies vaccination. I really hate needles.*

Another boom of thunder and Kevin looked towards his window. The lightning was causing shadows from the tree right outside to reach into his room like fingers. The candlelight flickered. He sent another text.

Beautiful Boy: *It sounds like Dylan was protecting you from something that really wanted to hurt you.*

He laid back on his pillow and closed his eyes. The scent from the candle comforted him. A lemon zest with evergreens and floral notes. The smell made him think of things sacred and holy. DING!

Tyler (the sorry jock) Glace: *I can't remember from what though. It must have been a bigger dog or bear.*

Kevin chuckled lightly and shook his head.

Beautiful Boy: *There are no bears here. It must have been a wild dog or something. You don't need rabies. You're rabid enough.*

A few moments passed by, and Kevin looked back at the photo of Dylan at Tyler's feet. He could tell the dog loved him. DING!

Tyler (the sorry jock) Glace: *Ha! Funny. I could have died!*

Kevin snorted.

Beautiful Boy: *It's just a scratch.*

Tyler (the sorry jock) Glace: *Is not! I could have lost a limb.*

Beautiful Boy: *So dramatic.*

Tyler (the sorry jock) Glace: *I'd have to walk around wearing a prosthetic for the rest of my life.*

Beautiful Boy: *Don't be such a baby.*

Another photo came through. Kevin tapped on it and couldn't help but smile as he gazed at it. Tyler had taken a photo of himself pouting and Dylan photobombing with his jaws open like he was laughing.

Beautiful Boy: *Cute.*

His eyes nearly bulged out of his face when he realized he sent that through. Oh, no! What if he reads too much into that?

Tyler (the sorry jock) Glace: *Dylan says thanks. You were obviously talking about him.*

Kevin huffed a sigh of relief and kept looking at the picture. Why couldn't this have been the Tyler he'd gotten to know? He could tell Tyler loved his dog to death.Another message came through.

Tyler (the sorry jock) Glace: *Why are you awake?*

He rolled over onto his side to get more comfortable.

Beautiful Boy: *The thunder woke me, and the power is out. No. I am not afraid of storms. I love them. That's when I saw your text.*

Tyler (the sorry jock) Glace: *Ah! I was wide awake when your text came* *through. Mom gave me some pain medication that should have knocked me out, but I'm wired.*

He didn't feel so guilty about responding to Tyler's photo now. But he could have been just saying that to make him not feel bad for waking him up.

Beautiful Boy: *Of all the people to show, why show me? We barely know each other.*

A few moments passed. DING!

Tyler (the sorry jock) Glace: *That's not necessarily true. I did pick on you for four years, which I am very sorry about, and we've had many classes together. I know what you look like when you're happy and I know what you look like when you're insulted. I know your favourite colour is blue and your favourite book is The Merro Tree.*

Kevin blushed. He remembered? He kept reading.

…Kylie is one of your favourite singers and Siouxsie and The Banshees is your favourite band. Your comfort food is Indian, but you want Mexican all the time. You collect crystals and you want to dance in the heart of a Sedona vortex. Oh! And your favourite constellation is the Pleiades. I do know lots of people, but I don't really have friends. I'm a douche.

Kevin reread the text four times. Even though the guy had been the very bane of his existence, his nemesis, he sure did know and remember a lot about him. Even though he bullied me, he listened to my conversations with Sara and remembered them. Some of this information was old. The bit about the Pleaides was from a get to know your classmate assignment from their freshman year. He hadn't spoken about that in a long time, let alone think much about it. It caused him to slowly remember how he had answered some of Tyler's questions. Things had been very different then.

Beautiful Boy: *You remember all this?*

A quick reply came. It was a paragraph. The guy was a very fast texter.

Tyler (the sorry jock) Glace: *I liked you. I liked you a lot. But…peer pressure and fitting in with the cool crowd. I hid myself under a lot of ugly colours. I'm not making excuses for myself. I know and accept I'm totally at fault. If I couldn't be your friend…I'd be your enemy. At least that way…I could keep…with you. I was messed up. Still am a bit. And by a bit, I mean a lot. Ever since you lashed back at me, I've been looking at myself, and making changes. I want to make it up to you. I'll do better. I'll be better. And I am sorry for hitting you in the face with my elbow. I hope your lip doesn't hurt too bad. It didn't look too bad at the party. Everyone was asking about you and me. It was kind of funny. Some even asked to touch my eye. They were impressed.*

Kevin touched his lip where Tyler had struck him. It no longer hurt as much as it did. The cream Mrs Davenport had given him was working wonders. Love and good vibes imbued every product she made.

He flipped backwards through his rolodex of memory and sent him a response.

Beautiful Boy: *Your favourite colour is green, and you don't really care much for books, but you do like magazines. Type O Negative is your favourite band and when you feel like being bad you eat Kentucky Fried Chicken with extra mashed potatoes and coleslaw. You like to collect sports memorabilia, and Whistler is your favourite place. Lyra is your favourite constellation because your grandmother played the harp at church. I don't really remember, but I think you told me something about her saying that was where God's music room was.*

He put his head down and closed his eyes. This was too surreal. Here he was having a conversation at almost four in the morning with his nemesis.

DING! It was a photo. Tyler was looking into the camera and smiling from ear to ear. It was the biggest smile Kevin had ever seen on him. Smiling or just looking genuinely happy really made his blue eyes shine. He could barely tell that his eye had even been bruised. Tyler was literally drop your pants gorgeous. DING!

Tyler (the sorry jock) Glace: *I'm going to make it all up to you, Kevin. I promise. I think I'm going to have to go to sleep now. The meds are kicking in. I can feel my eyelids getting heavy.*

Beautiful Boy: *I'm going to choose to believe you, Tyler. I am glad you're okay and thank you for your apology. Let's try and be friends from now on.*

He bit his bottom lip and decided to add… *Mainland accepted me as well. I have the next three weeks to accept their offer. We may be going to the same university.*

He tapped SEND. He waited to see what Tyler had to say. DING!

Tyler (the sorry jock) Glace: *That's awesome! Congratulations! If you do accept, it will give me four years to make everything I've done up to you. Thank you for accepting my apology. It really does mean a lot to me. Have a good…morning. At least you get to sleep in. I got to be up in two hours. TTYS!*

He crawled out of bed and walked over to where he was in the soft glow of candlelight. He tapped his camera and tapped the flip camera option so he could see his face on screen. Gazing at the candle-flame before him, he smiled.

The camera made a clicking sound and he looked at the picture. His left eye caught the flame, and his cheekbone was prominent. The other half of his face was hidden by shadow and his hair. SEND.

A few seconds ticked by, and a heart emoji appeared over the photo and Tyler sent him a kiss emoji blowing a heart. Kevin put his phone back on his nightstand and went to the bathroom. When he flushed, he heard the power come back on.

CHAPTER 11

Tyler's face brightened with a gentle smile as his gaze fixated on his phone screen, drawing him closer to his dog's side. Despite the throbbing ache in his left ankle, the soothing effect of the pain medicine began to take hold. Fatigue weighed heavily upon him, causing his eyelids to flutter, barely able to remain open.

Beauty had his emerald eye on him. He kept looking at the photo.

Just then, a familiar notification chimed on his phone, capturing his attention. His heart skipped a beat as he discovered that Kevin gave his kiss emoji a thumbs up. Dylan playfully licked his cheek. Kevin accepting his apology and that thumbs up instantly lifted the weight that had burdened his heart for months. Setting his phone aside, he closed his eyes, surrendering to the comforting embrace of slumber.

Before long, his consciousness slipped away like a fading candlelight, leading him into a dream illuminated by the soft glow of moonlight where he was chasing after a mesmerising eight-pointed star that was spinning just out of his grasp.

CHAPTER 12

He had dedicated the better part of the day to selecting the perfect outfit for his very first date. After much consideration, he concluded that a simple, yet tasteful attire would be the ideal choice. He opted for a fashionable denim shirt, complemented by a pair of dark indigo jeans. To complete his look, he adorned his feet with a sleek and polished pair of black boots that gave him two extra inches in height.

Approaching his dresser, he unveiled a cherished jewellery box, a souvenir from his visit to Montreal when he was fourteen. He delicately fastened his father's precious gift onto his wrist—a gleaming silver watch that held a special place in his heart. It was his most treasured possession.

Now came the hard part. What kind of cologne was he going to wear? Should he go with Versace? How about Thierry Mugler? There was always Jo Malone or Tommy Bahama. He could always go with his all-time favourite Tommy Athletics, but that was uber rare and he couldn't decide. Or there was Creed or Kilian. Oh, why did he have to have such a collection of fragrances? He was such a scent slut! What if he wore something Michael didn't like, and it totally turned him off? Then again, what if he wore something that really turned Michael on, and he was in danger of having his clothes torn off?

He looked over at his Arabian perfume collection and growled. He couldn't make up his mind. He loved them all. Okay, he said to himself. This is your very first date. Go with the scent you love most. DING!

He looked at the text from Sara.

Tommy Athletics it is. He spritzed it on himself and nearly swooned. It was an amazing scent. Soft and subtle in the beginning for a few hours and then it came raging back like a bull hours later. If he smelled this on a man, his brain would leak from his ears.

He gazed at himself in his mirror. I better not be catfished. He took a photo of himself and sent it to Sara. It was immediately surrounded by little pink hearts. DING!

Sara: *You look great!*

He quickly replied.

Kev: *Thanks!*

His mom stood at the door with the car keys in her hand. "Home by ten. You hear me? And if this guy turns out to be a sleaze, you put your phone under the table and call me. You don't have to say anything. I'll know what to do."

He nodded his head and hugged her. "Thanks, Mom."

"I'm trusting you," she said, and that was all the warning he needed. If he screwed this up, she'd never let him leave the house again. "Have fun and be safe. You got condoms?"

His head nearly exploded.

"Mom!" He yelled, snatching the keys from her with a quick swipe. "I doubt two hours is going to be enough time for something like that to happen."

"You never know," she said, laughing at him. "You may look at him. He looks at you. The next thing you know, you're in a restroom stall, or in the back of a pickup." She immediately glared. "Just not in my car."

"Ewe!" He rolled his eyes and headed out the door. "I'll see you at ten, Mom."

"Love you!" She called, waving from the porch. "Buckle up and drive safe!"

He got in the car, put his seatbelt on, slipped the key into the ignition, and turned it. He sat back in the seat and took a deep breath. Okay, he took a deep breath in, putting the car in reverse. Let's not screw this up.

CHAPTER 13

Intense anticipation swirled within Kevin. Beads of perspiration formed on his palms while his gaze darted repeatedly towards his watch. He was ten minutes early. Should he go in or linger a while longer, determined to make a grand entrance akin to the main characters in movies?

Joe's Pizza had moved into what used to be an old Pizza Hut, but Joe's had been around a lot longer. The pizza was better, and the locals didn't care for big chains. It wasn't the Blue Grotto vibe.

Eighties music was always playing, and the servers went around on roller skates. Nobody minded the old feel of Joe's Pizza because the amazing food spoke for itself.

Glancing back down at his watch, it was five minutes till eight. He had two hours to make a good impression or crash and burn like Flight S-666 straight to Hell.

He got out of his mother's car and locked the doors behind him with a BEEP and made his way across the street, dodging a couple and their cute puppy. Making his way inside, he was greeted by the voice of Tiffany singing "I Think We're Alone Now" over the speakers, and a girl he used to see in World Civilisations. The place wasn't that busy for a Friday night which immediately struck him as odd. Locals came here for drinks, chicken wings, and good company.

"Hi, Kevin," his former classmate greeted him with a big smile on her pretty face. "How are you doing?"

He greeted her with a small grin of his own. "I'm doing pretty good, Tanya. How are you?"

"I'm great!" She answered back, leaning across the counter. "Just earning some summer cash before I go away for college. Are you eating here, or do you have an order to pick up?"

"Dining in," he answered her, glancing back down at his watch. "I'm actually on a date."

Her eyes widened and began to sparkle.

"Really? Oh, thank God! I've been so bored. Are you here with Tyler? Everyone has been talking about the scene at Pete's party. Is it Tyler? Where is he?"

Gossip travels fast in this place.

"No," he shook his head, struggling not to blush from embarrassment. "It isn't Tyler. It's a blind date."

Tanya nodded her head. "Well, let me take you to your seat where you can have some privacy and I can spy without being seen."

Kevin was about to take issue with her statement, but she skated around the counter, grabbed him by the wrist and whisked him away.

"This is so exciting!" She nearly squealed, leading him along to a table in the far corner. "I'll get you some water and breadsticks while you wait."

She glided off and left him to sit in a daze. He looked down at his watch and saw that it was five past eight. He looked towards the doors to see them open. In walked a guy who looked to be a little over six feet tall. As the guy got closer and closer to where Kevin was seated, he was able to take in his appearance. Short dark hair, flawless pale skin under the lighting, a chiselled jawline that seemed to go on for miles, brutal red lips, and he appeared to be ageless. He could have been nineteen or thirty. In his hand, he held a single red rose.

"VermillionWings?"

The guy stopped a few feet from him and lifted the hand carrying the rose. "Rose Red?"

Kevin raised his hand in greeting. "Hi, Michael."

The guy smiled and it made his entire face look even more hand-some. Kevin could make out he had steel blue eyes and very white teeth. He was dressed like an Instagram model. His clothes fit him in all the right places. He suddenly felt severely underdressed.

Michael took the seat across from him. "Do I live up to your expectations?"

"You're not as tall as Tyler."

Kevin could smell him though. He knew that scent. It was Creed Aventus. The guy had excellent taste in cologne.

"Do I?" Kevin asked.

Michael nodded his head. "I knew you'd be cute, but I didn't realise just how much." He handed the rose over to him. "For a cutie."

Kevin felt his cheeks trying to burn as he graciously took the rose from him and sniffed it. He smiled at Michael and set it aside. The scent was amazing. Michael reached out and placed his larger hands over Kevin's.

"I'm serious. You're beautiful."

Kevin could feel the weight of those larger hands. Looking down at them, they were nice hands. They looked strong and the nails were perfectly trimmed and glossy. They reminded him of pink shells he'd found on the beach. But they felt cold, and it was a sticky night.

"And?" Michael asked, causing him to gaze back up at his stunning face.

Kevin made no move to extract his hands. The smell of Michael and his eyes were hypnotic. It was like he was slowly being sucked into them. A falling sensation.

"Here is your water, Kevin," Tanya said, gliding up to stop right before their table. "And the breadsticks I promised. They're fresh out of the oven. They're hot, but not as hot as your date. Jesus Christ! You are gorgeous!"

Kevin got his bearings and looked at her. "Huh?"

"This is too cute," She gushed. "Just look at how taken in our ice prince is by you. Let me get you two some menus and I'll bring you out some water as well."

Ice prince? He hadn't been called that in ages. The tsunami on wheels glided off.

Michael chuckled. "I like her."

Kevin nodded his head. "She was in a few of my classes during school. We were project partners a few times. She's always been nice to me. She's a good one."

Michael took those big hands away and Kevin immediately mourned the loss of contact. The bigger teen glanced around the restaurant and smiled. "This is a cute place. I like it. Old school."

Kevin agreed with him and then decided to give him a delayed response to his earlier question.

"You're more than what I expected," he answered the guy honestly. "I was expecting a sugar-daddy to come walking in dressed like he was twenty. I feel underdressed for this." He gave a self-conscious smile. "And thank you for your compliments."

Michael shook his head. "You're perfect. Now, where is that water? Did she have to go find a glacier?"

Kevin laughed. Time passed quickly. There were no awkward pauses or a loss for words. The conversation between them flowed effortlessly. Lots of laughter and playful little jabs here and there.

Kevin finished off his last bite of pizza and quickly apologized as he checked his phone. It was Sara checking in on him like they had agreed on. It was nine on the dot. He sent a quick reply.

Kev: *Going great. Check back at ten, please!*

He slipped his phone back into his pocket and watched Michael take the last sip from his frosted glass of Dr Pepper. The guy had eaten an entire large meat-lovers all on his own as to where he had just finished a small supreme with extra jalapenos. They were good pizzas!

The two of them talked a little bit more about everything. Books, movies, places they'd been. He'd even told him about Tyler and how things seem to be cool between them now. Michael had smiled, but it never reached his eyes when Tyler had been discussed. He quickly catalogued that as a no-go topic.

"It's a nice night," Michael said, placing his empty glass down on the table. The ice in it clinked together. "Would you like to go for that walk down to the beach? We have time before you need to get home."

Kevin reached for his wallet, but Michael held up his hand to stop him in the act.

"I'm paying," he said, pulling out his own wallet and slipped a crisp one-hundred-dollar bill into the leather check holder. He rose to his feet and held out his hand for Kevin to take. "Shall we?"

Kevin picked up his red rose and took that offered hand.

CHAPTER 14

Under a crescent moon, clouds drifted leisurely as the gentle surf crashed against the shore. Following Michael down the wooden ramp, they made their way towards the pristine white sand beach. A cool, salty breeze tousled his hair, while a few bats darted overhead.

Reaching the base of the steps, they decided to shed their boots and socks, leaving them behind by the stairs. With caution, he secured his rose in the safety of his left boot. The absence of people on a Friday night seemed peculiar, adding an air of intrigue to the evening.

Kevin's reservations faded away as he grew increasingly at ease in Michael's company. The kindness and attentiveness of the older teen had a calming effect on him.

Michael gently took his hand, and together they strolled side by side towards the water's edge, where the waves playfully caressed the sandy shoreline. Each step sent a pleasing coolness through his feet, and he revelled in the tactile sensation.

Every now and then, he caught the intoxicating scent of Michael, which set his pulse racing. It was a captivating blend of bergamot, rose, and ambergris, subtly infused with hints of lilac.

Suddenly, a rush of cold water washed over his feet, jolting him back to reality. With an unexpected yelp, he instinctively leaped backward, much to Michael's amusement. Hastily retreating from the advancing tide, he couldn't help but feel a surge of exhilaration mixed with a touch of embarrassment.

"Oh, no, no, no, no," he said, jumping and landing in dry sand. Michael laughed. He stood in the water. He didn't seem bothered by how cold it was at all. Those eyes were looking right at him, and Kevin felt as if they were looking into him as well. It was as if those eyes were seeing every part of him. Visible and invisible.

Michael walked towards him, and Kevin felt heat rising along his neck. The guy was a dream.

"See those dunes over there?" Michael asked, pointing.

Kevin turned to look. They were about a hundred yards away. He nodded his head.

"Let's walk that way," the taller teen said, taking him by the hand again. "And then I'll walk you back to your car. Can't have you being late. I want to see you again."

Kevin looked down at their feet and noticed that Michael's were about as white as the sand under them. If it hadn't been for his immaculate shell pink nails, they would have blended in.

"You must not get a lot of sun," Kevin whispered, placing his smaller foot lightly on top of Michael's. Through his sole he could feel the larger foot was cold as marble.

"I sleep all day," Michael laughed, wiggling his toes. "And work all night. It's how I afford to take a beautiful guy like you out on a date."

Kevin gazed up into those hypnotic dark pools looking back at him. Michael had placed that hundred-dollar bill in that check holder without asking for any change back. Their total had only come to forty-two dollars. He had made Tanya's whole night. A waitress' wage was pennies to the hour. They lived on tips. "You're generous," Kevin said, letting Michael lead him towards the dunes.

Reaching the dunes, Michael gently pulled Kevin closer and turned him around to face him. He put his large hands on the smaller teen's slender shoulders and gazed down with those magical eyes.

"I can be very generous, Kevin," he whispered. His breath

smelled just as sweet as he did.

The taller teen pulled him in close and held him under the waning moon as the ocean breeze whipped around them. Kevin breathed him in, and felt his knees go a little weak. He couldn't believe this was happening to him. Here he was, on a date, with a guy who was obviously into him.

His breath suddenly caught in his throat when he felt those brutal lips lightly brush against his neck. He tilted his head back and they moved feather soft along his throat. Shivers raced up and down his spine. He was thrilled and terrified.

"You smell so good," Michael breathed against his neck. "Divine."

Oh, thank the gods! Here I was terrified! Kevin closed his eyes and leaned into the embrace. Those dewy lips opened, and Kevin hissed when those white teeth gently grazed his soft skin.

"Please, don't leave a bruise," Kevin muttered, wrapping his arms around the taller teen's broad back. "I'll have to hide it with concealer and my friend will see right through it."

"Gotcha!" Michael chuckled. "You're so cute."

Michael was so gentle with him; he never felt those razor-sharp teeth. All he felt was warmth and comfort. He moved his hands up to wrap his arms around the back of Michael's neck.

Then he felt Michael stiffen and pull away rather abruptly. The guy was standing back holding the back of his neck with his hand. The look in those eyes were momentarily alien but was quickly replaced with warmth. Kevin wondered if he was just seeing things.

"Sorry," Michael quickly said, rubbing the back of his neck. "I think a sand fly, or a mosquito got me. Are you okay?"

Kevin nodded. "I'm fine. Do you want me to have a look?"

Michael shook his head. "I'm cool. What time is it?"

Kevin quickly glanced at his watch and his eyes went wide. "Oh, crap! It's 9:45!"

"We better get out of here then," Michael said. "Can't have you in trouble."

Kevin was suddenly lifted off his feet and Michael was carrying him in his arms. The guy ran as if he were made of wind and gravity had no power over him. It was as if they had arrived at the steps in a blink. Michael let him down and they picked up their belongings before quickly running up the steps. They raced along barefoot towards where Kevin had parked his car. He had his phone out dialling his mother.

"Hey!" He said, racing along with Michael right at his heels. "I'm running to the car now. I'll be home as soon as I can. I'm really sorry."

"Did you have a good time? "His mother asked him. "How did it go? Never mind. You can answer that when you get home. Buckle up and drive safe. I'll see you when you get home. Love you!"

"See you," he replied. "Love you too!"

He put his phone back in his pocket. He ran right up to the driver's side door, unlocking it, swinging the door open, and being mindful with his rose, he threw his shoes in.

A cough behind him caused him to quickly spin around. Michael was grinning at him.

"Um," Kevin stuttered, trying to retrace where he left his dignity. "Thank you for an amazing first date ever."

Michael sauntered up to him and pulled him into a tight hug. Kevin's eyes went wide when he felt a tongue lick his neck.

"Have a good night, Kevin," Michael said, kissing his cheek before pulling away. "Drive safe."

This is so unfair, Kevin's mind raged. Cinderella got until midnight. Kevin stood on tiptoe and pecked him right on the mouth. "Good night. Got to go!"

He practically dived into the car. Putting the key in the ignition and turning, he was greeted by the blasting of Kylie's, 'Say Something.'

Chapter 15

Michael stood in the stillness; his unwavering gaze fixed upon the receding glow of Kevin's taillights as they dissolved into the encompassing darkness. A grim shadow eclipsed his face, gradually erasing the radiant smile that graced his lips. He reached up, his hand finding the nape of his neck, where the touch of Kevin's watch had left its mark, a lingering reminder of their encounter.

In that fleeting moment, he had sampled the essence of the boy, a tantalizing flavour reminiscent of honeysuckle, intoxicatingly sweet to the point of inducing toothaches. Yet, his indulgence had been ruthlessly interrupted by the cursed caress of silver. The searing agony it unleashed, like a bolt of lightning, jolted him back to the reality of its formidable power, an unwelcome reunion with the torment it could deliver—a searing burn that could ravage his flesh.

Strong as a mountain, but so many weaknesses. The sun. Fire. The touch of silver. OCD. The boy would not be bruised though. His bitemark had been healed by the saliva from his tongue. This one had spirit. There was a spark in him that could ignite the world. He might just make the cutie a vampire.

He raised his pale, muscular arms up to the night's embrace. The shadows closed him round, hiding him from mortal sight. He whistled like the wind blowing through a lonely graveyard, and his bare feet left the earth as he took to the clouds on vermilion wings.

CHAPTER 16

Kevin wearily settled into his desk chair. His fatigue more pronounced than ever. Concern lingered in his mind, hoping that this weariness didn't mean he was falling ill.

Following a detailed account to his mother and offering apologies for his getting home fifteen minutes late, Kevin indulged in a hot shower. The cascading warmth of the water provided bliss from the cool night breeze that had chilled him earlier.

Nestled gently by his bedside, Michael's single rose graced a delicate vase. An array of raw rose quartz crystals encircled it, enhancing its beauty. A thoughtful gesture from his mother included an aspirin, crushed and added to the water, ensuring the flower's longevity for a while longer.

RoseRed: *Got home about thirty minutes ago. Had to apologize to Mom and take a hot shower. I am about to fall asleep. I am exhausted. Thank you again for an amazing night and for the flower.*

He sat back in his chair and closed his eyes. He put his hand to his throat and gently traced along where those lips had been. It had been like a dream.

VermillionWings: *It was my pleasure. Sorry you had to apologize. Hope you didn't get into any trouble.*

He tapped the keyboard for a few seconds before responding.

RoseRed: *Nope. Not in any trouble. Mom was cool about it. She was happy I called and told her what was going on before ten struck on the clock. She said I was very responsible and owning my mistakes.*

VermillionWings: *That's cool. Glad you're not in trouble. Let's exchange numbers. Now that I know you're not some psycho, I'd like to talk with you on the phone from now on, if that's okay with you.*

Kevin laughed. He was more than happy to hear that. He quickly responded with his number and his cell went DING. He brought up the text message and programmed Michael's name in.

Michael: *Hey you!*

Meal 42: *Hey back!*

Michael: *I'll let you go to sleep. Talk tomorrow?*

Meal 42: *Of course!*

Michael: *Good night.*

Meal 42: *You too!*

He got up from his chair and placed his cell phone on his nightstand before crawling into bed. Just as he got comfortable, he reached over and snatched his phone and quickly sent Sara a text.

Kev: *Amazing date! Michael is HOT. I think he's really into me. He wants to talk on the phone from now on. Will tell you more tomorrow. Thank you for looking after me. BIG HUGS!*

Just as he sent the text message to her, his phone chimed right in the middle. It was Tyler.

Tyler (the sorry jock) Glace: *Hope your date went well. Had my vaccinations today. Hurt like hell. My bite wound doesn't look as bad as it did.*

Kevin tapped on the photo to make it larger, and he zoomed in to get a better look at it. The wound looked nothing like it had the night before. The bite was scabbing rather nicely. It no longer looked angry and red. The boy had good genes.

Beautiful Boy: *Thanks. Date went well. Sorry your shots hurt. Your ankle looks SO much BETTER! You might even get a sexy scar to show off.*

He fluffed up his pillow so he could lay back and be comfortable. He was so tired. It was getting hard for him to keep his eyes open. The walk on the beach and his nerves must finally be catching up to him.

Tyler (the sorry jock) Glace: *Glad your date went well. Yeah. I was scared I was going to get gangrene and lose my foot. LOL.*

Kevin smiled at his screen. He knew the guy was being dramatic. He was glad he was going to be okay. Another text from Tyler came through.

Tyler (the sorry jock) Glace: *I got to go to sleep too. I can't sit up any longer. All the adrenaline, I think. Plus, those needles had me scared to death. HATE THEM! Anyway, have a good night, Kev.*

Kev? So, we're shortening each other's names now? Well, I can do that, too.

Beautiful Boy: *Good night, Ty. Don't let the Boogeyman bite!*

Tyler (the sorry jock) Glace: *Ha-ha-ha! Night!*

He put his cell phone away, rolled over onto his side, made himself comfortable, and closed his eyes. No sooner had he done that he was in the arms of the Sandman.

CHAPTER 17

Tyler drifted into a deep, restful sleep, completely drained from trauma. However, when he awoke, an astonishing surge of energy coursed through his veins, invigorating him to the point where he felt capable of conquering a marathon running backwards. It was a delightful surprise, and his parents, eager to seize the opportunity, planned to treat him to a lunch for graduating with good grades and getting into Mainland University.

As he stepped into the bathroom, Tyler flicked on the light, shed his clothes, and gazed upon his reflection in the mirror, utterly astounded. The remnants of a once-vibrant bruise beneath his eye had completely vanished, leaving behind no trace that it had ever existed. The transformation was astounding—he not only looked flawless but radiated an undeniable sense of well-being.

Seated on the edge of the bathtub, Tyler gingerly unravelled the bandage encircling his ankle, preparing to cleanse the area. To his astonishment, what he beheld surpassed even his dad's wildest expectations. The wound had healed so seamlessly that it appeared as though it had never existed in the first place. Tentatively prodding the previously tender spot, he discovered that not even a hint of pain lingered.

How was he going to explain this? Turning on the shower, he let the water warm up a bit, and stepped under the spray. His mom called from the other side of the door just as he was washing shampoo from his hair.

"Fruit salad is on the table. Want to get Mexican for lunch?" His stomach growled. "Sounds great!"

As he gazed down at his feet, he watched the soapy water spin around the drain. He knew Kevin worked at the local witch's shop. Maybe he would stop in and see him after lunch. He'd take his own car. Perhaps the two of them could hit the town after and hang out for a few hours.

He reached for the new bar of artisan soap and squished the whole thing between his fingers as if it had been a marshmallow. He looked at the mess he'd made of it and growled.

What the hell? That had been twenty-four dollars!

Chapter 18

Kevin quickly took note of Mrs Davenport's dwindling supply of amethyst and citrine. His gaze swept over the shelves, and he recorded that she was out of shungite, eye agates, moldavite, and herkimer diamond. He had just sold the last piece of rose quartz; Tarot Moon's most sought-after stone renowned for its ability to facilitate unconditional love. People adored rose quartz, using it as a metaphysical paperweight, bathing with it, and even keeping larger pieces beside them while sleeping.

The morning had been a whirlwind of activity, with Kevin ringing up ten sales since the early hours. Customers flocked to the shop for their crystals, incense, and weekend reading materials. However, the lunch hour was notably quiet, a brief respite before business typically picked up again around two.

A couple of regulars had stopped in for readings, scheduling appointments at ten and eleven o'clock. At noon, Mrs Davenport had hurriedly dashed out to drop off shipments at the post office, which was set to close at 12:30. Assuring Kevin that she would return around one, she left him in charge.

Kevin lit a stick of incense and nestled it in a holder, revelling in the fragrant aroma. Mrs Davenport always concocted her own special blend, a delightful mixture of white copal, frankincense, mastic, and myrrh. The ethereal sounds of Daemonia Nymphe filled the air, setting a soothing ambiance. Gazing at the faceless goddess statue with a gentle smile, he settled back into his seat behind the cash register.

His stomach emitted a faint rumble, a gentle reminder of his hunger, but he patiently waited for Mrs Davenport's return before indulging in his lunch. As soon as she was back, he planned to dash across the street and treat himself to a delicious taco.

The tinkling of the silver bell above the door alerted Kevin to the arrival of a customer. He turned his head to see Tyler strolling in, making a valiant effort to maintain a composed expression, despite being captivated by his stunning appearance. Today Tyler looked nothing short of breath-taking, his once-bruised eye healed, and his hair expertly styled.

Tiffany started belting out "You and Me" over the shop's speakers.

Kevin's gaze met Tyler's vibrant blue eyes, and a radiant smile illuminated the handsome features of the jock. Dressed in a light blue knit polo shirt, a pair of charcoal-coloured chino shorts, and stylish suede loafers, Tyler held a white paper bag and a drink, radiating an air of confidence and allure.

"Hey!" Tyler greeted, walking up to the counter and setting the white bag and plastic cup down. "I thought you might be hungry, so I got you two chicken tacos with some chips and salsa. I think this is a Mountain Dew." He took a quick sip from the straw and nodded his head. "Yep. That's a good Mountain Dew, too."

Kevin took a deep breath and his stomach rumbled for the much taller teen to hear. He looked at Tyler with huge doe-like eyes and babbled a big THANK YOU. He tore into that bag like it was an early birthday present.

Tyler laughed and watched in awe as he guzzled the food down his throat like a woodchipper being fed tree limbs. It was so good! He absolutely loved El Mexicana. They were the very best! It even has fresh cilantro! I could just die!

With a full mouth, he tried to talk, but ended up almost choking. He made hand gestures pointing down, and Tyler got the gist. Tyler walked around the corner of the counter and showed him his ankle.

There was a fresh bandage wrapped around it.

"All the blood made it look worse than what it was," Tyler told him. "The only thing I can remember is how bad it hurt."

He even put his head down to show him how his bruised eye had faded away. It was completely healed now. The little bald patch was barely noticeable because of the way he had his hair styled.

Kevin swallowed and took a big sip from his cup. "Wow. That's amazing. Those must have been some shots."

Tyler nodded his head and walked back around to lean on the countertop while Kevin finished off his last taco.

"You're tearing them up," Tyler laughed.

Kevin loved every bite. "Oh my god, thank you! I was starving."

"Mom and Dad took me there to congratulate me on getting into Mainland," he said, picking up a Chinese lucky coin and eyeing it. "And I immediately thought about you."

He thought of me.

Kevin smiled and cocked his head to the side. "Even if I had already eaten, I wouldn't have turned it down."

Tyler put the coin back into the money frog's mouth where it had fallen out. "I know."

Kevin took quick note of that. He knows how a money frog works.

Kerli started to play over the sound system. 'Spirit Animal.'

"May I ask you something?" Tyler asked, pushing back off the counter to stand at his full height, which towered over the smaller blond. He was so much taller than Michael. How did I ever get the upper hand?

Kevin nodded, finishing off the Mountain Dew.

"What are you doing after work?" He asked.

Kevin turned thoughtful. He was going to go by Sara's and gush all about his date, and then go home and wait for Michael to call, but that would be after the sundown. He didn't really have any set plans for his Saturday afternoon.

"Nothing," he said, shaking his head.

"Cool," Tyler said, picking up a book off the rack beside the counter. "Want to hang out for a while?"

"I get off at four," Kevin informed him. "But Mrs Davenport might let me go earlier if we're not slammed."

"Awesome. You have my number." Tyler winked at him and handed the book he wanted to purchase across the counter for him to take. "I want to get this."

Kevin took the book from him and looked at the title and price. The Shapeshifter. Ten dollars. It was a used book someone had donated.

"Interesting choice," he told him in honesty. "You'll have to let me know if it's any good. I may want to borrow it."

He took the ten-dollar bill Tyler handed to him. Since it was a used book, he didn't charge any tax. He slipped it into a paper bag along with the receipt and a bookmark and handed it across to him. Tyler's warm hand gently brushed along his fingers as he took the bag and it felt like electricity going through him.

"See you around four, Kev," Tyler waved as he walked backwards. "I'll meet you here."

Kevin gave him a small wave back. "I'll text."

Tyler's warm touch lingered on his skin. The bell jingled after him and Kevin was left with his chips and salsa to finish before Mrs Davenport returned. He couldn't seem to stop smiling. Tyler had remembered he worked here and had brought him Mexican food right when he thought he was going to pass out from hunger. He honestly couldn't believe it. Tyler was trying. He had a somewhat guy friend now. He felt happy.

The shop phone began to ring, and he picked it up, still smiling.

"Thank you for calling Tarot Moon. This is Kevin speaking.

How may I help you? Wait. What? Slow down, Mrs Long. I can't understand you. What? You just saw a werewolf pop a squat in your koi pond? But the sun is out. You sprayed it with your garden hose? Now there's a big hole in your fence? And you didn't call Animal Control? Well, what do you want me to do about it? No. We ran out of wolfsbane two weeks ago and the new shipment hasn't arrived yet. No. We do not carry silver bullets anymore. Not after that kid nearly lost an eye. Yes. The gun will explode. Science. It's apparently a thing now. I'll inform Mrs Davenport the moment she gets back. Okay, now. Stay inside your house. Lock your doors. Call Animal Control. Don't say werewolf! No! Do not say werewolf! People tend to act funny when that word is mentioned. Say very large dog and you're terribly frightened. That will make them believe you and get there faster. I don't think blowing chili powder in its face is going to do anything other than upset it. It might do more than just urinate in your koi pond if you throw your rolling pin at it. Yes. Say very large dog. You're frightened. Please come quickly. You're very welcome. Do not throw the rolling pin. No. Don't throw your walker. You need that when it's raining. What if it comes back before they arrive? Do what you do when that lovely Mormon family stops by. You maintain eye contact while slowly drawing the curtains. Okay. Bye now. Do not say werewolf! You, too. Bye."

Kevin put the phone down and sat back on his stool and blew his bangs out of his face. He started to laugh. It had finally happened. The poor thing had finally lost her mind.

The bell jingled and Mrs Davenport walked in. He jumped up from his seat and leaned over the counter. "Do I have a story for you! One guess as to who I just got off the phone with."

Mrs Davenport huffed and rolled her eyes. "Not again."

CHAPTER 19

He sent a text message to Tyler, letting him know that Mrs Davenport was letting him leave at three o'clock. As he stepped out of the shop, he found Tyler waiting for him on the opposite side of the street. He was leaning casually against the driver's door of his vibrant yellow Corvette. He was still wearing the same attire from earlier.

Had he been hanging out in town since stopping by the shop?

Without hesitation, Tyler beckoned him over, prompting Kevin to look both ways before running across to where the taller teen was waiting for him. Although downtown Blue Grotto boasted just three stoplights, it remained a busy street.

"Hi," Tyler greeted. "All good?"

"Where are you and Bumblebee taking me?" He asked.

"Genevieve," Tyler corrected him. "And Bumblebee is a Camaro."

He laughed. "Genevieve? That's a prim name."

"I thought we could drive around for a bit. Maybe stop and get some snacks." Tyler said, walking him around to the passenger door. He opened it up for him. "And we could stop by the park."

Park? The siren from Silent Hill went off in his brain.

Kevin cocked a brow as he got into the car. "Thanks."

Tyler shut the door behind him. The jock's car had that brand new smell to it, but he could also smell Tyler's cologne as he put his seatbelt on. He knew that scent. Versace, Eros. Lemon and Cedar. It was different than Tyler's usual mandarin and lime.

Tyler jumped behind the wheel and the car roared to life. Type O Negative playing over the speakers. It was one of Kevin's top five favourite albums. The album was called October Rust, because in the fall, the leaves change to rusty colours.

All the windows went down, and Tyler looked over at him as he clicked his seatbelt into place. The breeze blew through his locks and Tyler asked permission to ruffle his hair. Kevin slowly nodded. That big hand ruffled away.

"Did that make you happy?" Kevin asked, playfully swatting the large hand away.

The jock laughed as he put the left turn signal on, gazing into his side mirror. "Been wanting to do that all day. You got really soft hair."

Kevin sat back in his seat as Tyler pulled out of his parking space and onto the road. The engine purred as he switched gears, and down the road they zoomed to the sexy growl of Peter Steele singing Wolf Moon.

Tyler drove with one hand on the wheel. He made zipping and zooming in and out of what little traffic there was look like an art form. He knew the road like Kevin knew every item in Tarot Moon's stockroom.

They drove around town for about an hour, talking about anything and everything. Talking with Tyler was a bit like flipping through an open book. It really made him wish the two of them could have stayed friends for all these years.

~*~

"He picked you up and ran with you in his arms because you were going to be late?" Tyler asked, dipping a chip into some fresh made salsa, and crunching down.

Kevin nodded, making himself another steak fajita. He took the tortilla, dipped his knife into the sour cream and spread it all over. He did the very same thing with the guacamole. Spooning out some pico de gallo, he added it before the lettuce. Last he added the steak with onions and bell peppers.

"He was worried I'd get into trouble," Kevin explained to him, taking a big bite, and all the flavours exploded in his mouth. He moaned before swallowing. "He's a really fast runner, too."

Tyler smirked, taking another bite of his chicken califas. "I'm the fastest runner on the baseball team."

Kevin took a sip of water. "I know. I've seen you run."

Tyler grinned at him.

"You can't tell anyone I told you this," Kevin said.

Tyler suddenly became all ears and leaned in. "What?"

"A frequent customer called the shop in a frenzy earlier today."

He spoke in a low tone, looking over both shoulders and back at him. "She said she saw a werewolf relieving itself in her koi pond."

Tyler blinked. "Huh?"

Kevin nodded. "I know! That's the reaction I had! But she was totally convinced. Even asked for wolfsbane and if we supplied silver bullets."

"A werewolf?" Tyler whispered, putting down his fork, and reached to take a sip of water from his glass.

Kevin leaned in closer. "She told me she sprayed it with her garden hose."

Tyler snorted and nearly choked.

"Now she has this huge hole in her fence where it bulldozed through it," Kevin went on.

Tyler sat his glass down and his face turned thoughtful.

"I told her it must have been a really big dog," Kevin said, and then he looked deep into Tyler's eyes, seeing specs of silver in all that blue. "Do you think it might have been what attacked you?"

"I was just thinking that." Tyler shrugged, sitting back in his booth. "It was so dark, and I honestly don't remember anything except bleeding with my mom and dad fussing over me."

Kevin dipped a chip into some salsa. "Can you believe she actually sprayed it with a hose?"

"The logical thing to do," Tyler answered, nodding his head. "It was soiling her fish."

Kevin started laughing. He could see the scenario playing out in his head. "Picture it," he said, striking a pose. "Little old lady shooing away a scary werewolf with her garden hose."

Tyler started laughing with him and mimicked a granny voice. "Get out of my yard!"

"I know!" Kevin laughed, looking at the empty salsa bowl and frowned.

"You want more, don't you?" Tyler asked.

Kevin nodded. "Always."

"Do you think Mrs Long's fish will become werekoi now?" Tyler looked at him.

~*~

Tyler pulled off the road and into the park. Kevin started to feel a little nervous about allowing himself to be brought here. This was where all the school jocks liked to hang out, practice and fool around with things other than extracurricular. He gazed out the window and saw a few younger kids playing basketball, and a set of girls playing tennis.

There weren't even that many cars. What the hell is going on? I know it's only the beginning of summer break, but this place should be packed. It's a Saturday night for Christ's sake! Where is everyone?

"Okay," Kevin said, turning away from the window to look at the

Rose Red

other blond. "Don't you think something funny is going on?"

Tyler glanced over at him for a second before putting his eyes back on the road. "What do you mean?"

"This is the park."

Tyler nodded.

"It's a Saturday evening."

Tyler nodded again.

"Where is everyone? Is there a concert? Did someone die? Did everyone suddenly leave town? It's been weird since yesterday."

Tyler shrugged his broad shoulders and pulled into a parking spot right next to the baseball field. He looked over at Kevin. "I've not really thought about it, but now that you say it out loud, it feels kind of spooky because town was unusually quiet today."

They both removed their seatbelts and stepped out of the car. Kevin followed him towards the gate. "Aren't you going to lock your car?"

Tyler shook his head. "We're just going to be right here."

Kevin put up his hand. "Oh, no. You're locking the car. I've seen one too many scary movies."

Tyler laughed and locked his car with a BEEP.

"Happy?" He asked.

Kevin nodded. "I always check the backseat before I get into my mother's car."

Tyler held the gate open for him. "Urban Legend?"

Kevin laughed. "I know it's stupid. I can't help it."

Tyler led the way across the empty fields towards a dugout, pulling a second set of keys from his pocket. Kevin followed him down into the dugout towards a big white door at the end. The taller teen unlocked the door and turned on a light inside. Kevin saw bats, balls, uniforms, a nice collection of whistles, and other things sporty and not a part of his reality. Can't relate. "Hold out your hand," Tyler said.

The jock handed him two wooden baseball bats. One was large and heavy and the second one was smaller and lighter. Tyler pulled up the bottom of his shirt. Kevin couldn't help but notice his well-defined abdomen and how it was covered in fine golden hairs. The jock was placing baseballs into the pouch he had made from his shirt.

He followed Tyler from the room and back out onto the field. The taller blond ran out to the pitcher's mound and dropped the balls at his feet and bent over to pick one up.

"Okay!" Tyler said, taking his place on the mound. "Take your bat and stand at the home plate."

Kevin pretended to be ignorant of how baseball worked. He had read books where the girl fell in love with the school jock. He was the basketball captain. He was the football star. Oh, he was the soccer king. He's the Prince of Baseball.

Kevin slowly made his way over and stood at home base and held up his bat like he was about to break some stereotypes.

"Wow," Tyler said, nodding his head. "You actually look like you know what you're doing. Count me surprised."

Kevin pursed his lips and parted his legs a little to feel more balanced and steadier.

"I had a feeling you'd be a righty," Tyler chuckled and pitched the ball at him lightning fast.

Kevin felt the air from it as the ball whizzed right by and struck the caged metal fence behind him. He didn't even get a chance to blink, let alone swing the bat.

"Um," he said, looking at the jock who was doing his best not to laugh. "Can we try that again? I wasn't ready."

Tyler picked up another ball and pitched it.

Kevin swung the bat as fast as he could. The tip of the bat connected with the ball, sending it flying over his head and to the right.

"If a player was behind you, and he or she caught that, you'd be out," Tyler said.

Kevin nodded, giving his bat a few practice swings while Tyler reloaded. "One more time."

Tyler tossed the ball up into the air, caught it, took his stance, and threw it.

Kevin swung the bat as hard as he could. He felt the bat connect and the ball soared over Tyler's head and bounced between second and third base, rolling beyond.

"Not a bad hit at all," Tyler clapped with approval. "Depending on the other players and how fast you can run, you may have made it to first without them catching it."

Kevin twirled his bat, only for him to lose it and it fell to the ground with a dull clang. "I meant to do that." He struck a pose. "I'm a star!"

Tyler rolled his eyes, and he ran towards him. "My turn."

Kevin held up his hands. "I've never pitched in my life. What if I hit you in the head?"

"Good thing I have a very hard head," Tyler joked, picking up the larger bat.

"Your funeral," Kevin snorted, running towards the pitcher's mound. He picked up a ball and held it tight in his hand. He'd never done this before in his life. Hell, he hated playing with a beachball in the pool. He turned towards Tyler to see that he was already in his familiar stance.

He had a fierce look on his face. He took this sport stuff very seriously.

"Ready?" Kevin asked.

"Yep!" Tyler said.

Kevin focused on the spot he had once read to focus on when throwing a baseball. He took a deep breath and released it upon pitching. He threw as fast and as straight as he could.

Tyler swung the bat like he was defending his life. The bat connected with that ball and sent it soaring. Kevin spun around to see it fly over the fence.

He turned back around to look at the jock. Tyler looked just as surprised as he was.

"I've hit the fence plenty of times," Tyler said, looking very pleased with himself. "But I've never hit it over the fence. Let's do it again."

Kevin picked up another ball. He focused on that spot and threw the ball. The ball went soaring over the fence again. Tyler looked even more pleased with himself.

"Do your run," Kevin told him. "Show me how fast you are."

"When you hit a homerun like this," Tyler said, taking off at a jog. "You don't have to run fast. You're meant to be cocky and show off."

"You told me you were the fastest runner on the team," Kevin teased, watching him saunter towards first. "Prove it."

"Okay," Tyler said.

Kevin watched as Tyler picked up speed very quickly from first to second and then it was like he was the roadrunner from a Looney Tune cartoon. He was leaving dust in his wake as he ran from second to third and came slamming into home like a lightning strike.

"YEAH!" Tyler roared as his feet stomped down on the home plate. "How was that for you? Fast huh?"

"When you get to Mainland, I think you should add track to your resume as well," Kevin told him, clapping his hands. He was very impressed. The guy could run.

Tyler picked the bat back up. "Come on. Throw me another one."

Kevin put his hands on his hips. "You're just going to knock it over the fence again."

Tyler swung the bat. "One more, Kev."

Kevin bent down and picked up another ball. He held it tight in his hand and began to focus on that spot again. He drew in a deep breath and without realizing, he threw it with the speed of a comet.

Tyler swung so fast and so hard the baseball exploded on impact with the bat, cracking the wood. Kevin ducked, putting his hands up to shield his face. Tyler dropped the bat and fell backwards, losing a shoe as debris from the baseball fell around him.

He looked just as shocked as Kevin felt from his seat on the ground. The guy had just exploded a baseball and cracked a solid wooden bat. Kevin blinked and realised he had stopped breathing. He drew in a big breath and let it out.

"YOU ARE AMAZING!" He yelled, running over to him. "YOU JUST MURDERED THAT BALL!"

Tyler's shock quickly turned into the goofiest look Kevin had ever seen on his handsome face.

"I guess," he said, getting to his feet with Kevin's help. "All these late-night practices and working out more has paid off."

The taller blond gazed down into Kevin's eyes and smiled. It was the softest smile Kevin had ever seen on him.

"You think I'm amazing?" Tyler asked barely above a whisper, like he was having trouble believing him. Kevin bent down at the jock's feet and picked up the remains of their dearly departed baseball and held it up to him. "You just did this. Of course, you're amazing. I'm not surprised Mainland snatched you up. You've always been good with sports."

"But," Tyler said, lightly placing his hands on Kevin's shoulders. "You think I'm amazing?"

Kevin looked at the remains of the baseball, feeling the weight of those strong hands. How in the hell had he bested Tyler in their classroom brawl?

"You've changed. You're actually trying to be a better version of you." Kevin said, playing with the destroyed leather, not meeting his eyes. "You used to be the bane of my existence and now look at us. You bring me food to my work, we drive around town together, eating out, and now you have me on a baseball field. I've never swung a bat in my life, let alone actually hit a ball thrown by an actual pitcher. You're doing what you said you were going to do. You're being a better you. So, yes. I think that's amazing. I think you're amazing. A lot of people speak the speak, but don't sissy that walk."

He was shocked when Tyler suddenly pulled him forward into a tight embrace. The big jock was hugging him. He could feel the heat radiating from him like he was a furnace and the scent of him was amazing.

Tyler pulled back a little and leaned down. He placed a gentle kiss on his cheek, and that smile, it was the most beautiful smile he'd ever seen.

"I have a confession to make," Tyler said, giving his shoulder's a gentle squeeze.

Oh, no. Here it comes...

"I've watched RuPaul's Drag Race as well."

Kevin blinked and then laughed out loud. DING! He quicky pulled his cell from his pocket. He looked at the time. It was going on six. The text was from Sara.

Sara: *Where are you?"*

"Do we need to go?" Tyler asked.
Kevin nodded.
"Let's put all of this away and I'll take you home," he said.
Kevin picked up the jock's shoe and blinked. It was a big shoe. It was a size 13.
"Thanks," Tyler said, taking it from him, and slipping his bare foot into it.
"Could you do me a favour?" Kevin asked.
Tyler looked at him and nodded.
"Will you drop me off at Sara's?"
"Sure."
Kevin smiled and sent Sara a text.
Kev: *On my way.*

CHAPTER 20

Tyler masterfully maneuvered the car to a halt at the curb, right in front of Sara's big house. The engine's gentle purr faded into the background as Peter Steele's song, 'Haunted,' played on.

Kevin unbuckled his seatbelt, turning his gaze towards the athlete. Tyler's eyes were fixed upon Sara's residence, leaving Kevin curious about the hidden thoughts dancing within the taller blonde's mind.

As if tuned into Kevin's curiosity, Tyler, with a hint of intuition, slowly shifted his attention to meet Kevin's inquisitive stare. A radiant smile adorned his chiselled face, emanating an aura of sheer contentment.

"Thank you," Kevin said, giving him an equally warm grin.

Tyler nodded.

Kevin moved to get out of the car, but Tyler gently put a hand on his arm to stop his departure. The smaller blond turned back to look at him.

"What?"

Tyler was biting his bottom lip. "Are we friends now?"

Kevin blinked. "Are we?"

"Yes," Tyler told him matter of fact. "We are friends now."

"The kind of friends who kiss each other on the cheek?" Kevin asked with a cocked brow.

Tyler nodded again. "We're posh like that."

"Yes," Kevin laughed. "Yes, we are."

Tyler grinned from ear to ear. The jock then turned away and opened his car door and got out. Kevin's eyes followed him. He isn't. And he is... Tyler walked around the front of Genevieve and opened the door for him. Kevin graciously accepted, but Tyler wasn't playing as dumb as he sometimes pretended to look.

"What?" He asked, putting on a very serious face. "I can't have you putting fingerprints on the wax job."

Douche bag! Kevin playfully punched him in the shoulder. It was like hitting a brick wall. Those muscles were hard as stone.

Tyler laughed. "Have a good night, Kev. Thanks for hanging out."

Kevin held his hands at his side. "Good night, Ty. Thanks for the food and showing me how to hit a ball and throw one for that matter. It might come in handy one day."

"Text me when you get home?" Tyler asked.

"I'm not going to get lost," he said.

"Too many scary movies," Tyler winked. "Remember?"

Kevin rolled his eyes. "Get out of here before the neighbours start asking questions."

Tyler waved and Kevin watched him drive off before making his way up to Sara's door. He didn't even get the chance to knock when the door swung open. Sara grabbed him by the front of his shirt and pulled him inside.

"OH. MY. GOD." She spoke. "I. WAS. WATCHING. FROM. THE. WINDOW. TELL. ME. EVERYTHING. BITCH."

~*~

"Okay. Unwell lady and incontinent werewolf aside," Sara said, waving all that goss away for the time being. "Your date went well. AND TYLER KISSED YOU!?! Tyler Glace?"

Kevin sat back on her bed. "My cheek. He kissed my cheek."

"He fucking kissed you!" She said, giving her chair a good spin around for dramatic effect. "Your nemesis. Your bully. The very bane of your cosmos. He kissed you! I fucking knew it! My gaydar is never wrong!"

He felt his cheeks beginning to burn.

"This is insane," she said, shaking her head. "The end of senior year and you have a college aged guy and your nemesis gunning for your goodies."

"Michael is really sweet," Kevin said, staring off rather dreamy eyed. "He has this magnetism that pulls me in."

Sara was looking at him like her eyes just turned into lips smacking their chops. "And?"

"Tyler knows me," he said, looking away from her intense stare. "I don't think he wants me like that…I think he just wants a friend. A gay bestie."

"Bitch, please!" She said, throwing a stuffed unicorn at him. "I saw him get his fine ass out of his car and open the damn passenger door for you. The passenger door! Like I just told you, my gaydar is never wrong. A friend does not do that. Hell, when was the last time I opened any door for your ass? Never."

"I open the door for you," he interjected.

"That's different!" She snapped. "I'm a lady. You're supposed too! Plus, you're not trying to stuff my honeypot."

Kevin shook his head. "You're crazy. There is no way Tyler likes me like that."

"Oh, I'm crazy?" She asked, rising from her chair. "Let me tell you a little something about crazy, Mr Rose. Crazy is when you beat the shit out of your high school bully and that bully falls dick over ass in love with you. It's classic really. He has secretly liked you all these years and picked on your ass until you finally did something about it. Boys and girls do this all the time. Boy likes girl, so he pulls her hair and puts worms in her backpack. Girl likes boy, so she kicks his nuts up into his empty head and embarrasses him in front of his pals. They date, have a baby, get married, and hate each other happily never after and the kid grows up to be a life coach and gives crystals to all his clients."

Kevin let her words enter his ears and dance around inside his brain for a few moments. It had been three days and Tyler seemed like a completely different person. A complete one-eighty.

"Okay," Kevin said, sitting back up, and placing the stuffed unicorn upright in his lap. "Let's say you are correct, and Tyler is what you say...what do you think I should do?"

She tossed her hands up and fell back in her chair.

"That's entirely up to you." She told him, rolling the chair over closer to him. "You could lead him on and make him slowly suffer for all the years of hell he put you through or you can see where this goes just by being yourself and letting it all happen organically. You're going to be eighteen soon. You are going to have your pick of hundreds of gays and bisexuals when you start university. It's all just beginning. Your entire life isn't choosing between two guys who have the hots for you. Fuck their feelings and their boners. What do YOU want?"

Kevin just looked at her with wide eyes. Who the hell was this girl and what had she done with Sara?

"This is about you," she pointed hard at him. "And what you want."

When had she become so wise and the voice of reason? It was like he was looking at his girlfriend for the very first time. He felt his eyes begin to tear up. She really did care about him.

"What?" She asked, suddenly looking very concerned and moved closer to him. "What did I say? Was I too blunt? Maybe I shouldn't have smoked."

"No," he said, making room for her and letting her hug him tight. "You just...I've never felt wanted...you know...desired to be dated before."

"Oh, Sweetie," she said, hugging him close. "You are one of the most beautiful boys I've ever seen. When you get to Mainland, all the rainbow boys are going to be slipping into your DMs lubed and ready."

He laughed. She was so crass!

"Come on," she said, pulling him up to his feet. "I'll take you home."

"Do you really have to leave for Miami tomorrow?" he asked.

"I don't have too," she said, grabbing her car keys from a bowl sitting by a statue of the Three Graces. "But this six-week internship at my aunt's design studio is going to look really good on a resume."

"Send me some sand," he told her. "And some sea glass."

"Honey," she said, leading the way down the stairs from her room. "I am going to create something truly amazing for you to wear. Petshop of Horrors style."

He grinned. "Bring me back some sea glass anyway."

She pushed him out the door. "About this werewolf…were you serious? Was it really peeing in her koi pond? Will the koi become werekoi now?"

CHAPTER 21

Kevin entered his bedroom, distracted by a whirlwind of thoughts. Before collapsing onto his bed, he sent Tyler a text message, letting him know he had made it home. He sank face-first into the soft pillow. During his contemplation, an elusive fragrance wafted into his senses—a ghostly scent of jasmine that mingled with his fading rose. A few petals had blackened and fallen off. Realising the ineffectiveness of the aspirin he had put in the vase, he sat upright, his gaze sweeping across the room, searching for something that didn't belong.

Suddenly, it became undeniable. The air was saturated with the unmistakable essence of freshly cut jasmine. His eyes were immediately drawn to a vase positioned in the centre of his dresser. An abundance of pure white blossoms radiated their delicate fragrance. He did not recognise this vase. He didn't know where his mom was and immediately sent her a text.

Moon Child: *I like the jasmine. It smells great. Thank you!*

He kept looking at the vase as if a spirit had entered his room to snatch him.

"You're welcome!" She called from downstairs.

Oh, thank God! He sank onto his soft bed, surrendering to its comfort, and released a sigh. Was he beginning to lose his mind? He pondered. Perhaps it was Tyler's indulgence in cannabis at the party—a concoction he unwittingly inhaled one too many times. It could

explain the illusory fragrances of jasmine, and even projected a terrifying reflection of himself in the bathroom mirror.

Yet a lingering uncertainty clung to his thoughts. Didn't he
catch a whiff of jasmine prior to Tyler's appearance? Could the effects
of marijuana manifest in such ways? He was not a weed doctor. He
didn't know and he couldn't remember now. A witch's cackle drew him
from his thoughts. He pulled his cell from his pocket and looked at the
screen. It was a text from his boss.

The Witch: *Hey! Can you mind the store for me tomorrow between 10 and
noon? I must sort this whole thing out with Ella. She has utterly convinced
herself that a large cryptid was refilling her koi pond and wants an entire
property cleansing. I don't think I have enough olive leaf, bay leaf, juniper,
lavender, frankincense, cedar, rosemary, and myrrh. I'm still waiting on that
wolfsbane. Maybe I can substitute mugwort. If she's not careful, all this anxiety is going to attract djinn.*

Kevin started laughing all over again. Mrs Long's property was
big. She was going to need a lot of herbs and resins to cleanse that
place. He hoped Mrs Davenport would charge her properly this time.
The good stuff was costly. Especially the frankincense and myrrh. The
shipping and handling and the import tax just kept going up.

Rainbow Scream: *Sure thing! I don't mind at all. I'll see you a little before
ten.*

A cool breeze ruffled his curtains.

The Witch: *You're the best! Also, would you mind stocking the display case
with some new necklaces I got in?*

He was more than happy to do that for her. It meant he would
get first dibs on anything he liked.

Rainbow Scream: *You bet! I love having first dibs.*

He quickly set a reminder in his phone, so he'd get up in time.

The Witch: *You love that discount. See you tomorrow. Good night, Kiddo!*

Rainbow Scream: *Good night!*

He put his phone down and walked over to his computer to check if Michael had sent him any messages. As he was clicking through and scanning a few things, his phone began to ring. Michael! He ran over and snatched up his phone and took a deep breath before tapping the bright green circle.

"Hi," he greeted, sounding more put together than he felt.

"Hello," that deep voice said from the other end. "I'm calling to speak with Kevin. Is he around?"

"Ha!" He laughed. "I don't sound that different."

That chuckle caused his skin to break out into goosebumps. The guy's voice did things to him.

"How are you?" Michael asked him.

"I'm good," he answered, taking a seat at his desk. "How are you?"

A yawn. "I just rolled over. About to get me a little some-thing-something to perk me up."

Kevin smiled. The two of them talked for what felt like forever. Taking his phone away from his ear, he saw they had been talking for about forty-five minutes.

"A werewolf?" Michael asked, and Kevin put the phone back to his ear. "That's…interesting."

"You're telling me," Kevin agreed.

"Are you doing anything tomorrow night?" Michael asked. "I'd really like to see you again."

Kevin instantly began to feel his heart flutter in his chest.

"I have no set plans," he said, leaning towards his desk, and flipping pages of an old textbook as loudly as he could. "But I think I should be able to pencil you into my schedule."

Michael laughed. "How does 7:30 sound?"

Kevin sat back in his chair and put his feet up on his desk. "Sounds great!"

"Text me your address and I'll swing by and get you," Michael told him, over what was a very loud cracking sound.

"What was that noise?" Kevin asked.

"Oh!" Michael said, giving him that delightful chuckle. "That was my neck and back. I stretched all the way out."

"Sounded like a bone breaking," Kevin laughed. "Are you okay?"

"All good here," Michael answered him. "I'm going to have to get up and get myself in the mood for work. Have a good night, Kevin. See you tomorrow night."

"Hope work goes well," Kevin told him. "Have a great night, too."

"Bye."

"See you."

He put his phone down on his desk and looked up at the ceiling and smiled. He was going on a second date with Michael. The guy wanted to see him again. Oh. My. God. He's coming here to get me. Ohmygodohmygodohmygodohmygodohmygod! He's coming to my house to get me! AHHHHHHH!

After collecting himself, he sent Michael his address. Michael sent him a thumbs up. He got up. He needed a shower.

~*~

Sixteen Candles held a special place in his heart as his all-time favourite movie. What captivated him was the authentic portrayal of the characters, each simply embracing their lives without the burden of stress or consequences. Among the many memorable moments, one scene stood out above the rest—Samantha's exit from the church, only to find the handsome Jake waiting for her. Witnessing Samantha's sheer shock and joy upon seeing Jake never failed to ignite his own excitement, no matter how many times he watched it. Plus, Samantha's sister's wedding was hilarious. Love the teapot.

As he prepared to settle into bed, he turned off Netflix, allowing the satisfaction of the movie to linger. Just as his eyes were about to surrender to sleep, the sound of a bat connecting with a ball alerted him to a text message from Tyler.

He rolled over and reached for his phone, bringing it up to his face. Although he had contemplated changing the name in his phone, he decided to keep it as Tyler had initially programmed it.

Tyler (the sorry jock) Glace: *Sorry for the delayed response. Glad you got home safe. Thank you for spending the afternoon with me. Let's do it again soon.*

He smiled to himself. Today with Tyler had been fun.

Beautiful Boy: *You're welcome. Yes. Let's.*

Tyler (the sorry jock) Glace: *Goodnight, Kev.*

Beautiful Boy: *Goodnight, Ty.*

He gently placed his phone aside and turned onto his side, gazing at the gentle sway of his curtains. Gradually, his heavy eyelids started to droop, as if lured by the soothing dance of the fabric.

Faint murmurs seemed to caress his senses, but his eyelids weighed too heavily to grant him a glimpse of who or what was speaking. A blissful warmth enveloped him, coaxing him deeper into sleep. It felt as though he were drifting away on a billowy cloud, weightless and serene. Finally, the Sandman claimed him.

C HAPTER 22

Tyler beamed with contentment as he gently placed his phone beside him on the bed. His mind was consumed with the incredible speed at which he had raced around that field and the sheer power it took to destroy that baseball. The memory of Kevin's astonished expression lingered in his thoughts, along with the tender sensation of their brief embrace. It was a stark reminder of the time they had squandered, the potential of their friendship left untapped.

He could still feel the sensation of the smaller boy's smooth cheek on his lips. The smell of his soft skin.

Determined, Tyler crossed the expanse of his bedroom until he reached the closet door. Opening it, he revealed a lengthy metal rod he used for securing weights. With anticipation coursing through his veins, he hoisted the solid steel rod into his grasp, feeling its weight and strength. A surge of curiosity enveloped him. Just how strong am I?

Taking a slow deep breath in, Tyler positioned himself at the centre of the room. His hands grasped the solid rod, extending it horizontally in front of him. As he exhaled steadily, a sense of calm washed over him. Focusing his energy, he tightened his grip and gradually began to bend the rod with a remarkable ease, as if it were pliable like string cheese.

Fuuuuuuuck… His eyes widened. This thing is solid steel! What is happening to me? The rod contorted into a U shape before crashing onto the floor with a resounding bang. He instinctively recoiled, gazing bewilderedly at his own hands as though encountering them for the very first time.

"What did I tell you about dropping those weights, Ty?" His dad yelled from downstairs.

"Sorry!" He called out, still looking down at the bent metal.

He was abruptly startled by the faint murmurs escaping his father's lips, echoing beside his ear as though the man were right next to him. Startled, he swiftly twisted around with a startled yelp, only to find his bedroom door tightly shut. The room remained void of any company; he was utterly alone. I must be tired or I'm turning into Superman. Inhaling deeply, he made his way over to his desk and sank into the chair. With a few clicks, he logged into his laptop and initiated the melodies of Heart.

Allowing the music to transport him, he closed his eyes, leaning back in the chair, relishing in the nostalgic tunes. Suddenly, he propelled his chair forward, rolling across the floor, and swiftly grabbed his cell phone from the bed. Unlocking the home screen, he prepared to take a photo of the metal rod in front of him.

Twirling around in his chair, he swiftly captured a photograph of the distorted steel lying on the floor. The urge to share the image with Kevin compelled him to access their texts, but he hesitated.

He anxiously nibbled at his bottom lip, sinking deeper into the chair's embrace. Sliding his thumb across the screen, he revealed a picture of the beautiful boy amidst a bower of dewy red roses, their thorns lurking within all that sweetness. You're beautiful, Kev.

He rose to his feet once more, striding towards the bent steel. Carefully, he retrieved the twisted metal and concealed it amidst the depths of his closet, cleverly camouflaging it beneath a mound of dirty clothes. His insistence on handling his own laundry diminished the likelihood of his mother stumbling upon it, preventing any pesky questions as to why he had just destroyed an expensive piece of gym equipment.

As he quietly shut the closet door, a sense of having another secret washed over him. He needed to distract himself. He swiftly seized his new book from the desk. Settling down upon his bed, he made himself comfortable, only to end up rolling his eyes and getting back up with a grumbled curse under his breath. He needed to pee.

CHAPTER 23

Breakfast was a fruit salad, crafted with a medley of yummy ingredients. Among the ensemble were dates, purple dragon fruit, crisp slices of red apple, a perfectly ripened banana, a generous handful of fresh goji berries, all crowned with a cascade of golden passionfruit nectar.

Kevin took his seat at the table, his spoon poised, dipping into the golden passionfruit. A smile adorned his face as the tiny seeds burst on his tongue, releasing an explosion of flavours in his mouth. It wasn't his normal breakfast of bacon and eggs, but he wasn't exactly feeling normal.

He kept staring over at the waste bin where he'd dumped his dead rose. It hadn't lasted very long.

His mom came into the room and greeted him with a wave. "Am I dropping you off?"

He put the spoon to his mouth and nodded.

"Mrs Davenport is so good to you," she said, looking around for what he assumed were her keys. "Am I picking you up after?"

He shrugged his shoulders. "Not sure. Tyler may want to do something after. I have another date with Michael tonight."

She stopped her search and looked at him. "Really?"

"He's coming by to pick me up at 7:30," he said, getting up to carry his empty bowl to the sink.

She followed him into the kitchen. "Must be serious then."

He grinned and turned around to her. "I hope so."

"Just be careful, Baby," she said, stepping up to give him a hug. "I lucked out with your dad."

"I will be," he assured her, so happy he had her full support in this adventure. "You didn't raise a dummy. Should anything happen, I have 911 on speed dial and…" He was going to say he would call Sara, but she was in Miami for the next six weeks living the high life. "I'll call you and Tyler."

"I still can't believe the bully is your friend now," she said, letting him go and looking at him. They were the same height. "You must have knocked some good sense into him."

Kevin nodded. "Taste. I knocked taste into him."

"Come on," she said, running her fingers through his hair. "Let's get you to work."

He picked up his mom's purse and followed her out the front door.

~*~

Kevin turned the serene spa tracks on, filling the room with tranquillity. He arranged a cluster of blessed prayer candles upon the sacred altar, their gentle glow casting a soothing aura. Before the enigmatic statue of the faceless goddess, he delicately positioned a fragrant incense stick, imbuing the space with an ethereal fragrance.

Navigating past a collection of essential oils adorning the shelf, he made his way towards the counter. There, he discovered the box of necklaces entrusted to him by Mrs Davenport, awaiting their rightful display within the gleaming glass case.

Suddenly, a jolt ran through Kevin as the air conditioning unit hummed to life, startling him. His eyes instinctively glanced upward, observing the Tibetan prayer flags swaying in response to the air currents. The sound of the air conditioning always made him think the roof was about to lift off the building.

I am never going to get used to that. Picking up a pink boxcutter, he carefully slit the cardboard box open. Inside was probably over a hundred necklaces in cloth bags. This was the type of thing he lived for. Finding treasures.

Carrying the loaded box over behind the display case, he got down on his knees. He put it down beside him and slid the glass doors open and started sifting through the necklaces for the best ones to put out.

There were pentacles with garnets and a few with lapis. He discovered a few Thor's hammers and crescent moons with rainbow moonstones. A few Celtic crosses scattered throughout with peridot. He placed them one by one in the display case, setting them up so they caught the best light. Each one was made of sterling silver. Mrs Davenport didn't do pewter. She said something about the energy was all wrong.

As he reached the bottom of the box, his hands fell on something that instantly caught his attention. The necklace in this cloth pouch had some weight to it. He opened the pouch and took the necklace out. It reminded him of the Hand of Fatima or the Hamsa, but the name it was tagged with had Hand of Ishtar written on it with a graceful script. The eye in the centre of the palm was made of purple tourmaline.

Unclasping the silver chain, he placed the pendant around his neck. He got up off his knees and walked over to the mirror that was behind the statue of the faceless goddess. It looked good on him. He really liked it. Gazing down at it, he lifted the Hand of Ishtar up and gazed into the purple eye. Looks like I found the one I want.

He gazed into the mirror, his lips curling into a smile. However, the smile quickly vanished as his reflection stared back at him from the depths of the gilded glass. It was his own face, and yet it seemed somehow different, unsettling. Then it became terrifying.

The complexion of this face was as pale as delicate moth wings, and its eyes shimmered with a vibrant, molten violet hue. The alluring red lips were tainted by a black liquid that gleamed with a captivating golden sheen.

Slowly, he took a step back, distancing himself from the bewitching mirror. As he did, he noticed the golden locks surrounding his doppelganger's face gently swaying in a breeze he couldn't perceive. Each strand of hair radiated an inner light, casting a halo-like glow upon his head, akin to a crown woven from golden serpents. This was far scarier than Touched by An Angel.

His reflection placed a shimmering palm against the glass. The whole frame began to vibrate on the hook. It was going to fall off! The silver bell above the shop door jingled, causing a raw terrified scream to tear its way from his throat and he spun around throwing the boxcutter like it was a ninja star.

CHAPTER 24

A concerned voice was speaking to him.

"Kevin!"

He trembled uncontrollably, the very ground beneath him seemed to shift as if the floor and ceiling had exchanged positions. His head throbbed with a tightness, and his vision became distorted, as though he was peering through water. He reached out in search of something solid, teetering on the edge of collapse. Just in the nick of time, a pair of strong arms took hold of him before he could fall.

"Kevin?" The voice asked him, slowly lowering him down.

"Kevin!"

The voice. Familiar.

"Kevin."

Tyler…

He caught that familiar scent as he took a breath in. Versace, Eros. Lemon and Cedar. He focused on that scent, breathing in deep. Trying to ground himself. Breath in two-three-four-out-six-seven-eight. Blinking his eyes a few times, he found himself gazing up into Tyler's very concerned face. The bigger blond was holding him. They were both down on the shop floor. Tyler had him in his lap.

"Tyler?" He managed to ask. "What are you doing here?"

"You sent me a text," the jock said, putting the back of his hand to Kevin's forehead like he was feeling for a fever. "Are you okay?"

"I did?" He asked, liking the touch of that large hand very much.

"Yes," Tyler answered him. "You said you wanted to ask me something in person."

It took him a moment to remember what it was he had been doing. That was right. He had sent Tyler a text during the drive over.

"Can you stand?" Tyler asked him. "What was that just now? You looked scared to death…and that scream…"

Kevin nodded his head and Tyler gently and slowly helped him to his feet. Tyler kept an arm around him, helping to support him until he found his legs again.

"Thank you."

He felt so grateful Tyler had been there to keep him from seriously hurting himself. Then he looked up at the jock in horror.

"Did I throw boxcutters at you?"

Tyler nodded. "I dodged."

His cheeks burned full crimson-gold. "I am so sorry. I could have hurt you!"

Tyler chuckled. "The blade isn't even an inch long. You'd have to be a ninja to kill someone with one of those just by throwing it."

Kevin cringed. "I am a purple belt."

Tyler helped him over to a chair in the small tea area. "Lucky for me you're not a blue belt."

Kevin managed to laugh at that. "Thank you for catching me."

Tyler gently squeezed his shoulder. "Do you want to tell me what that was about?"

Kevin ran shaking hands through his hair, noticing how extra gentle the large blond was being with him. "I saw my doppelganger in the mirror…again," he pointed towards the altar.

Tyler looked to where he was pointing and then back at him. "What do you mean? Like you saw another version of yourself?"

Kevin told him everything. He told him about the jasmine that was there and then wasn't while attending Pete's graduation party. He told him about the face looking back at him in Peter's bathroom mirror that was his face but wasn't his face. And he told him about what just happened a few moments ago. Tyler was looking at him.

"You think I'm crazy," he said, putting his face down in his hands.

"No," Tyler answered him, kneeling in front of him and placing a hand on his shaky knee to stop it. "I did see a ghost when I was eight years old, and I was attacked a few nights ago by something I can't remember seeing. So, you're not the only one who has, or is, experiencing weird stuff. I mean...you do work in a witch shop."

Kevin looked between his fingers at the large hand resting on his knee that was no longer shaking. "You're not wearing your bracelet."

"Oh!" Tyler said, taking his hand away and rubbing his naked wrist. "For some reason it started breaking me out. My dad said one can develop allergies to certain things over time."

Can one become allergic to silver? Kevin sat back in the chair and took a few deep breaths. "I don't know what's going on. Last night, when I was drifting off to sleep, I thought I heard whispering over my head, but I couldn't open my eyes."

Tyler stood up. "Let me get you some water."

Kevin pointed towards the checkout counter. "There is a little fridge behind there. It should have a few bottles of water. Clients tend to get thirsty after their Reiki sessions."

He watched the jock. Tyler was wearing a crewneck tee, a pair of slim fit chinos, and white sneakers. The bandage was still around his ankle. He heard the fridge open and close, and Tyler came back with bottled water in hand.

"Thanks," Kevin said, taking it from him.

He popped the cap and drank half the bottle right there and then.

"Are you okay?" Tyler asked him again, taking a seat.

"I am now," Kevin nodded. "Thank you."

Tyler smiled. "Not to change the subject of what's been happening, but what did you need to speak to me about in person?"

Oh, you know. I just wanted you to call me every hour on the hour to make sure I'm still alive while on my date with Michael tonight. Nothing too strenuous. Would you mind?

He couldn't ask that of him now. He'd just have his mom do it. Tyler was being such a…hero right now.

"I'm going to ask Mrs Davenport if I could have a session with her when she gets back from seeing Mrs Long about her werewolf fiasco and I wanted to ask you if you would be my support?" He said, feeling like a complete idiot now.

Tyler's whole face was taken up by his amazing grin. "You trust me that much?"

"You've been pretty amazing these past four days and you did just save my life…or the very least kept me from getting a very serious concussion." Kevin told him, taking another sip from the cold bottle. "So, yes. I want to trust you this much."

"Okay," Tyler said. "Yes. I was just going to go to the park and hit some balls, but this sounds far more interesting."

"Dressed like that?" Kevin asked.

"I have a change of clothes in Genevieve," Tyler said, looking away from him. "I put this getup on for you." He scratched his chin.

Kevin blinked.

Tyler immediately put his hands up. "I know you're dating this guy and it seems you like him, but that doesn't mean I can't be another option at some point."

An option?

"This isn't fair to you," Kevin immediately said. "I don't want to do anything that's going to make you feel like this friendship we're building is leading you on…"

Tyler shook his head and smiled. "I've been such a dick to you… and if this guy hurts you in anyway…"

Kevin held his breath. Tyler really was trying to redeem himself.

"You really are trying to change," he whispered.

Tyler looked at him with those amazing eyes. "I like you, Kevin. I've always liked you. We may not have the sports thing in common, but we really do have a lot in common."

"I wish…" Kevin said under his breath, turning away from that aqua gaze. "I wish things had been different…"

"I know," Tyler agreed, sitting back. "Me too."

"I have a date with Michael tonight," he said, turning back to look at him.

Tyler nodded. "I am feeling jealous, but that's my fault."

"The real reason why I asked to see you," Kevin went on. "…is that I don't feel at a hundred with him yet. I…uh…I wanted to ask if you'd text me every hour and check on me…and if I don't answer… you call the cops."

Tyler blinked. "You really do trust me."

Kevin nodded. "I know you're not a bad person, Tyler. You were just going along with the IN crowd."

"Yes." Tyler said. "I'll do it. You can trust me."

"He's picking me up at 7:30 at my house and I'll send a photo of his license plate."

Tyler slapped his knee, laughing. "Wow! I love you!"

Kevin smiled.

"What were you doing before all the weird stuff happened?" Tyler asked.

"I was putting necklaces away in the display case over there," Kevin pointed. "And I found this one that I really like," he said, showing it off to him.

Tyler leaned forward and reached across to touch it. He held it between his index finger and thumb. He smiled. "It suits you."

"You think so?"

Tyler nodded and let it fall gently back against his chest. "I don't think I've ever asked, but does this shop have a restroom?"

Kevin stood up. "I'll show you where it is."

CHAPTER 25

The restroom door closed behind Tyler, and he leaned his broad shoulders back against it, his heart pounding in his chest. He raised his hand and examined his index finger and thumb, their skin raw and pink from the burn caused by Kevin's pendant.

As the book had described, silver had become an irritant during his metamorphosis. The bracelet his dad had lovingly bought for him could no longer adorn his wrist. Any contact with silver now sent a searing sensation through his skin, making even holding a spoon during breakfast impossible.

Each new revelation served as undeniable evidence that he was no longer the person he used to be. From now on, he was going to have to use bamboo utensils for eating and only wear 24kt gold.

Pushing away from the door, he made his way to the sink. He turned on the faucet, letting cold water cascade over his minor injuries. He held his finger and thumb beneath the refreshing flow, feeling the burning sensation gradually subside. When he turned off the tap and examined his digits in the light streaming through the small window, he found the rawness completely healed.

Staring at his reflection in the mirror, a look of wonder crossed his attractive visage. It wasn't just him experiencing these strange occurrences. Kevin was going through them as well. Reaching for a paper towel to dry his hands, a smile played across his lips. Perhaps he could never have Kevin in the way he yearned for but having him as a friend meant everything. It was far better than not having him at all, and certainly an improvement from the way things had been before.

With newfound resolve, he opened the restroom door and walked out.

"Do you need help with anything? Do you want me to put some of these hippy clothes on and pose in the window? I'm sure I could lure some tourists in." He said, striking a pose.

The beautiful boy looked at him and laughed.

"We just got this magazine in about haunted sports stadiums around the world. You want to read this while I finish getting this place looking presentable for tomorrow?"

Kevin handed him the magazine and Tyler looked the cover over before taking a seat again.

"Do you want some tea or coffee?" Kevin asked him. "I can put the kettle on."

"Tea." Tyler said.

He had never liked the smell or taste of coffee.

The smaller teen nodded.

"We have this entire assortment. Matcha, rose, jasmine, passion fruit, apple, honeysuckle, pomegranate, hibiscus, black tea, and blueberry that's harvested in Whistler. "I'll pour you a cup of hot water and you can have your pick. On the house."

"Blueberry," Tyler told him. "Whistler is my favourite place."

"I had a feeling you would pick that one," Kevin said.

Tyler smiled after him and began to flip through the magazine.

CHAPTER 26

Mrs Davenport entered the shop at half past noon. The two boys engrossed in their reading lifted their heads in unison, acknowledging her presence. Kevin, his face radiating warmth, welcomed her with a smile that spread across his lips. He closed his book and gently placed it upon the polished counter.

"How did it go with the property clearing?" He asked.

She was looking from him to Tyler and back at him again. "When did this happen?" She asked pointing from one to the other.

"Four days ago," he answered her, hopping off the stool. "Well?"

"She was riddled with anxiety the whole time I was there," she said, putting her basket down behind the counter and Kevin fetched her a fresh cup of rose tea. "And you should see the state of her garden fence. Whatever it was tore right through it."

"A bear?" Tyler asked.

Mrs Davenport shook her head. "No bears here, Dear. Well, not the ones you're referring to anyway."

Kevin snorted, bringing the teacup over to her. Her joke went over the jock's head, which was rather impressive, because he was way taller than most. The guy could reach up and touch the ceiling without trying. Tyler gave him a confused look and Kevin mouthed tell you later.

"I apologise for the lateness," she said, taking the cup of freshly brewed tea from Kevin with gratitude. "She was in a right state."

"It's all good," he told her, taking a seat in the chair beside Tyler. "You know I love my role here and I am more than happy to come in whenever you need me."

"I can see you found a necklace you like," she said, pointing with her spoon at his chest.

He placed his hand over the silver pendant and smiled. "Yep. Hand of Ishtar."

"It's yours," she said, giving him a nod. "My way of making up for having you come in on your day off."

"Oh, no," he said, shaking his head. "This is worth more than the two hours I've worked. It's sterling silver and purple tourmaline."

She held up a hand to him. "Two and a half hours and I'm paying you for those as well."

He didn't know what to say. This was so nice and generous of her.

"Say thank you," Tyler told him, giving him a wink.

Kevin nodded his head at her and grinned from ear to ear. "Thank you."

She sat back and took a sip of her tea. "This is lovely. We must get more of this."

Kevin tried to get his thoughts in order, because they were all rushing around behind his eyes. He allowed her to enjoy a few sips of her tea and get comfortable.

"Mrs Davenport?" he asked.

"Hmm?" She said, placing the bone China teacup down on the round table in front of her. She gave him that look she always gave him when she knew something was up.

"I have a rather big favour to ask you," he said, looking from Tyler and across the table at her.

"Oh?"

He nodded and took a deep breath.

She cocked a brow at him. "I can tell something has got you bothered. I felt the energy when I walked through the door. Something with the mirror behind the Goddess?"

His eyes widened and he told her what was going on. She crossed her legs and made herself more comfortable as he filled her in. Her eyes got curiouser and curiouser the more he shared. There was something else in her eyes, but he couldn't read their meaning.

"I see," she said, looking from him to Tyler. "And you couldn't see this ghost jasmine?"

"No," Tyler shook his head. "I could only smell it."

"And your face in the mirror," she looked at Kevin. "It was your face, but not your face?"

He nodded.

"And the whispering last night," she continued. "Could you understand anything being said?"

"No," he answered her. "They were speaking softly, and it was another language."

"Could you recognize any part of it?" She asked.

He shook his head.

"No. I've watched a lot of foreign films and tv shows. I even doubt Siri would be able to identify this language."

She tapped her chin with a painted nail. There was a set of Lenormand cards on the table before her. She began to flip a few of the gilded cards over.

He watched as she flipped over nine cards. A set of three in three rows. Left to right.

MAN - HEART - MAN
BOUQUET - CROSSROAD - EIGHT-POINTED STAR
HOLY BOOK - KEY - MOUNTAIN

Her brow creased. She then flipped over two more cards. It was the scythe over the fanged serpent's head.

She sat back and looked right at him and then over at Tyler beside him. She reached for her cup of tea and took a sip.

"What does that mean?" Kevin asked, pointing at the cards.

"The first line needs no deep explanation because it clearly shows two men who are in love," she said, looking right at him. "The second row indicates one who is gifted being led towards the divine."

Kevin felt a chill rush up his spine. He snuck a glance over at Tyler who was leaning forward, looking right at the cards on the table in front of them.

"And the third line?" He asked.

She looked as though to be weighing her options on a scale he couldn't see or even begin to fathom. "Secrets coming forth which will open a door that could never be stopped from opening to begin with."

He swallowed.

"And if you look at the first line going down, this shows one man who has many secret gifts. The second line going down shows the heart divided between a choice, but the key is there to open the way. It is saying listen to your heart. It will guide you."

"And the third line going down?" Tyler asked.

Mrs Davenport took a deep breath and let it out slowly. "The second man…it shows him unleashing the divine within."

Tyler sat forward in his seat. The bigger blond looked highly interested in the reading now.

"And what about this line?" Tyler directed with his finger.

The man, crossroad, and mountain.

Mrs Davenport nodded. "He has a choice to make. Go his own way or be patient and follow the divine."

Kevin sat back in his chair. He was about to ask another question when Tyler pointed again.

"What about the scythe card over the snake card?" He asked.

"The snake indicates danger. A threat. The scythe is almost always a warning. Since the scythe is over the snake's head, it means the danger can be diverted or defeated."

Tyler reached over and squeezed Kevin's shoulder without looking at him. It was an automatic reflex to comfort. It instantly made Kevin feel good. His heart did a little loopedy loop.

He cleared his throat. "What about what happened earlier?"

Mrs Davenport took her eyes away from the cards and looked right into his eyes. "I can do a psychic scan and see if something has attached itself to you."

He nodded his head. "Let's do that."

"Okay," she said, rising to her feet. "Let's lock up for the day, turn this music off, and get you prepared. I can't have you flipping out and throwing sharp objects at our customers if you have a gift developing."

Kevin and Tyler both got to their feet to help her.

"Thank you so much!" Kevin said, completely meaning it.

She gave him a warm smile. "This is what I do."

"Come on," Kevin said, grabbing Tyler by the arm, leading him after Mrs Davenport.

CHAPTER 27

Mrs Davenport ushered them into her Reiki Room, conveniently situated just across from the room dedicated to spiritual readings. With an air of authority, she directed Tyler to settle into the plush wingback chair nestled in the distant corner, ensuring he had an unobstructed view of the proceedings and was well enough out of the way. Kevin thought he exuded a regal aura, like a prince seated upon his throne, ready to address his subjects.

Turning her attention to Kevin, she kindly requested him to remove his necklace, as well as his shoes, fostering a deeper connection to the sacred space. Standing tall, she instructed him to extend his arms gracefully by his side, embodying a posture of openness. He watched as she ignited a smudge stick composed of her own homegrown olive leaves, lavender, and rosemary. The fragrant tendrils of smoke wafted gently over him, guided by a delicate fan crafted from the iridescent feathers of turkeys and adorned with opaque black tourmaline. All the while, she whispered sacred prayers under her breath, her words weaving a shield of spiritual protection around the space, like an intricate, slowly swirling cone of energy.

He took note of Reiki symbols painted across the walls. Runes of protection painted across the ceiling above their heads. Charms to ward off negativity dangled over the massage table.

"Okay," she said, coming back around to face him. "I want you to lay down on your back on the table. I am going to place black tourmaline and shungite all around you."

He climbed up onto the bed and laid flat, making himself comfortable. He had no idea how long this whole procedure was going to take. A few moments passed.

"I am going to light some special incense," she said. "It is a mixture of frankincense, myrrh, copal, mastic, and sandalwood. This will further purify and help make this a safe space to do what we want to do."

"All right," Kevin said, focusing on the Eye of Medusa above his head. The charm had been used for thousands of years to ward off the evil eye and other malicious intent. Mrs Davenport had gotten it while on a trip to Cyprus.

"I want you to close your eyes and take a few breaths in and out slowly," she instructed him.

He closed his eyes and listened to her telling him to breathe in and out in a pattern that helped slow his heartbeat and cause him to enter a deeper state of relaxation. She then told him she was going to beat on a drum to help disperse some of the stagnant energy around him. Vibrations of a sacred nature purified and cleansed. She wanted him to focus on the drumming and relax deeper and deeper.

He wondered what Tyler was thinking about all of this. It really was amazing that the jock was willing to go along with this just for him.

"Focus, Kevin," Mrs Davenport's voice spoke over the steady beating of the drum. "I can feel your mind wandering."

"Sorry," he whispered.

He broke out into sudden goosebumps when he felt her blow a gentle breath against his third eye chakra and again at his crown chakra. It caused him to shiver.

Okay, Kevin. Focus on the drumming. Listen to the beat. Follow the beat down, down, down, down... Don't think about Tyler. Don't think about Michael. Just breathe in that sweet-smelling incense and focus on the beating of that blood moon red drum. Don't think about how sexy Tyler looks or how amazing he smells. Don't think about how dreamy Michael's voice had sounded over the phone. Just focus on that beating drum. Boom. Boom. Boom. Boom. Boom.

The more he listened to it, the more it began to sound like a heartbeat. Boom-Boom. Boom-Boom. Boom-Boom.

Another soft breath was being blown against his third eye and once again at his crown. He followed the beat further down, until he suddenly opened his astral eyes and found himself in a space where there were endless doors. Was this right?

He looked ahead, his gaze unwavering and filled with anticipation. Casting a lingering look behind him, he allowed his eyes to roam, absorbing every detail. His gaze then shifted, traversing the realm of possibilities as he surveyed both upward and downward, taking in the grand spectacle before him. It was a tapestry, an ethereal galaxy of doors that seemed to stretch into an aurora borealis of infinity. The spaces between were littered by spiralling stars.

Within this boundless expanse, an assortment of doors whispered to him, each with its own unique character and allure. There were the resolute wooden doors, emanating a sense of strength and tradition. Vibrant and meticulously painted doors infused the scene with splashes of vivid hues, capturing his imagination. Ornate doors, adorned with intricate designs and embellishments, whispered past tales of opulence.

His eyes took notice at the centre, and he started running. It was a giant door and it glowed from within. This massive door was the very heart of his spiralling universe. It appeared to be the very nucleus that held the entire cell together. The gravity of himself. It was the beginning. The very beginning. His beginning. Am I supposed to be here?

No matter how fast he ran, the door never seemed to come any closer. He stopped running. Door after endless door. It was all moving. Dancing to that heartbeat. A kaleidoscope of HIM. He reached out with his hand and opened his mouth. Come to me.

Time and space shifted like rolling waves of shooting stars. That giant door was suddenly right in front of him. It was titanic in size. Designs carved into that brilliant blue lapis lazuli were primordial. Images and script that had no meaning to his modern brain.

The light coming from around the edges of the door made him think there must be some great star within. The very stone pulsed as if it were keeping something contained. The intricate carvings began to glow violet bright. He reached out and touched the icy stone that burned with a cold fire. The current of energy coursed through his spirit body and pierced his essence with millions of needles filled with a bliss that could only be described as rapturous.

He was suddenly standing in the centre of an almost perfect square room. The walls, floor, and domed ceiling were pulsating with a soft pearlescence. It was as if looking at a field of opals under a full moon. He took a deep breath and the air smelled of sweet amber and rose. The very air glittered and sparkled as if made of wisps of crystal shards in mist.

He slowly turned around and a powerful hand gripped him by the throat. He gasped and was shocked to be staring into his own face. The vision before him was a cosmic terror. It was him, a vision of perfection in every aspect. Not a single flaw or imperfection marred his glistening, flawless alabaster complexion. The lunar lights danced upon his impeccably carved cheekbones, as if they were delicately chiselled from the rarest gemstone. His radiant violet eyes glowed with an intensity that suggested an inner universe, captivating and mesmerizing all who beheld their dreadful gravity. And his resplendent, coiling locks appeared to be forged from precious metal, each strand imbued with an ethereal luminescence. They formed a halo of molten gold, crowning his head with divine elegance.

The hand enveloping his throat possessed a strength capable of either holding the world or crushing it into powder, yet it caused no discomfort or pain. And when he spoke, his ruby lips, glistening with a touch of golden ichor, formed words that transcended mortal speech, resonating with a voice that was otherworldly, captivating him with its celestial beauty.

A beauty so overwhelming and irresistible no human ear could withstand such vibration. It was many waves smashing through stone and lightning burning up the earth.

It's time, his perfect doppelganger spoke in words that caused him mortal pain. Time for US to WAKE UP.

If this was the real world, those eyes would boil away entire oceans. This face would launch a thousand nukes.

That hand tightened around his throat, and he gasped as he felt himself being thrown backwards through what felt like epochs crashing into eons. Force and pressure pulled and squeezed at him from every direction. He was being torn apart and he screamed as the earth came right at him all big and blue and spinning.

He hit the surface with a BOOM that shook the foundations of the very elements. His eyes snapped open with a crackling hiss, and he found himself gazing up at a giant crack across the ceiling and all the painted runes were smoking because they had been burned.

Drawing in a deep breath, he sat up to see that the crack went right down the wall splitting it. It was as if a pair of great hands had tried to rip the room apart. Something trying to escape or make a simple point.

They can't contain US. HA. HA. HA.

He quickly turned his head and looked behind him. Mrs Davenport was peaking around from where she was standing behind Tyler.

My what big eyes you both have.

"That was not supposed to happen." She spoke.

The Reiki symbols along the walls looked as if they'd been scratched at by great hands with even sharper nails.

He raised his finger, slowly pointing up. "Did I do that?"

They both nodded.

"Kevin," Tyler whispered. "Your eyes…"

The glass Eye of Medusa fell, nearly hitting the top of Kevin's head. The charm bounced off the massage table, hit the floor, and shattered into several sparkly blue pieces, causing him to wince.

Mrs Davenport huffed. "I need a fucking drink."

CHAPTER 28

Kevin stood before the statue of the faceless goddess, captivated by his own reflection in the mirror positioned beyond her form. With a sense of profound horror, he peered into the looking glass, discovering the remarkable transformation in his appearance.

Gone were the familiar sea-green hues of his eyes, replaced by a mesmerizing shade of violet. Unable to tear his gaze away, he became lost in his reflection, observing himself through new eyes.

With each passing moment, his fascination and terror grew, as his countenance underwent a remarkable metamorphosis. His features appeared altogether different, as if sculpted by the hands of Aphrodite, creating a visage that was both unfamiliar and yet undeniably his own.

"And Mrs Davenport started wafting this giant fan made from peacock feathers at you," Tyler said, and Kevin watched him from in the mirror throw his hands up in the air. "And BAM! The room went full-on Poltergeist. It was incredible! I can't believe I didn't record this."

Kevin stared back into his new eyes.

"It wouldn't have worked," Mrs Davenport said, walking out of the Reiki Room with her cell phone in hand. She held what remained of it up for the two of them to see. "My new phone, as you can see, has been melted. So much for at least having audio."

"I am so sorry," Kevin said, turning to her. "But my eyes. I can't go home like this. What will I tell my mom?"

"You can stay with me until we figure something out," Tyler offered him. "My bedroom is big."

Kevin gave him a small smile. It was very sweet of him to offer.

"Contacts," Mrs Davenport said. "All you kids wear them now."

Tyler snapped his fingers. "Genius. Contacts. Sara always wears them."

Kevin walked by them and back into the wrecked Reiki Room. He had to take it all in once more.

"I did this?"

Unbridled chaos had been unleashed within. He put a hand up to his throat as he gazed around. Her poor room was going to need a whole new everything. As he took a closer look, he noticed what had once been her healing lemurian crystals from Mount Shasta had all turned back and shattered. Even the black tourmaline and shungite was broken. He was going to have to work full time plus weekends without pay for the next ten years in order to pay for all of this. He was never going to own a car or a house.

Mrs Davenport stepped up beside him with a glass filled with something far stronger than tea. He felt Tyler standing close behind him. Warmth radiated from the taller teen.

"I was meaning to refurbish this room at some point," she said, taking a big drink from her cup. "Now I have the perfect excuse to get started early. I've put it off for too long."

"I am so sorry," he gushed. "I'll work for free from now on. I'll be your indentured servant. Please don't tell my mom!"

"Oh, hush your head!" She said, slapping his shoulder. "I've seen spirits, witnessed weird lights in the skies, felt things nobody else could… and now you've…"

He felt Tyler's big hands on either side of his shoulders, giving him a gentle squeeze. "I'm lucky to be alive right now. You could have killed me back in homeroom."

Kevin placed a smaller hand on top of Tyler's right one and squeezed back. "How come you're not running and screaming out the door?"

"Because this is the coolest shit I've ever seen!" he said, laughing deeply. "Screw being a medical doctor or a nurse. I may go into parapsychology while I play baseball. I can't believe this is actually real."

Kevin turned around to look up at him. "Are you serious?"

"Turns out I'm not just into sports, Kev," Tyler said, ruffling his hair. "Ever since I saw that ghost... but this... wow!" He pulled Kevin into his arms and squeezed him tight against his broad chest.

The smaller teen got a whiff of him and nearly swooned. The mix of body heat and his cologne. The guy smelled too good.

"Okay," Mrs Davenport said, looking through her wrecked room at what could be salvaged. "Kevin, here's your necklace. It looks like it was the only thing not annihilated."

He graciously took it from her and placed it around his neck.

"And your shoes," Tyler said, picking them up for him.

Kevin thanked him and slipped them on.

"This means I'm going to get that fountain I've always wanted to install," she said, gazing around with her hands on her hips. "And from now on, sorry Kevin, this room is going to be off limits, okay, Hun?"

Kevin nodded with huge eyes. "Understood."

"And we tell nobody about this," she said matter of fact. "None of what just happened is to leave this shop. Insurance and all that."

Both boys nodded at her.

"All right," she said. "I am closing up and going home. You can come in tomorrow after the insurance people leave and help me clean. Tyler, you can help too. We will need those large muscles of yours."

"Of course," Tyler said, flexing his arms.

He did have amazing arms.

"I'll be here," Kevin agreed.

She waved them both off.

CHAPTER 29

As both boys left Tarot Moon, Mrs Davenport released a breath she hadn't realized she had been holding. Running her trembling hands through her hair, she made her way to the counter and took a seat. Her gaze wandered around the shop, and she let out a long sigh.

The mere act of his "mild" awakening had sent tremors through the ethereal ground beneath her feet. Had she been negligent in her warding and protective spells, he could have flattened the entire shop. She still had shivers. The Lenormand never lies. The deck always spills the tea. This had been her biggest fear. It was happening again. Just like it had almost two decades ago. Kevin was almost eighteen. Just like his dad had been. She looked towards the statue of the Goddess. How am I going to tell his mother, Lady?

Chapter 30

Kevin followed Tyler out to his car. Like him, the jock was also full of surprises. He was sure Michael would run screaming out the door into the night after all that woo-woo, but Tyler had not. The taller teen was fully embracing this wild experience.

Michael! His date!

"Let me take you home," Tyler said, opening the passenger door for him. "And I'll be sure to leave before this guy shows up."

"What?" Kevin asked, stopping before getting in. "You think I should still go? I just nuked my job. I've got zero credit for life. I'm seventeen and so deep in the red. Can one get any deeper in the negative? I didn't take accounting. I don't even know how it works. Debit? Credit? Jesus Christ!"

Tyler held out both hands in front of him to try and instil calm.

"What I think you should do and what I'd like for you to do are two very different things," Tyler said matter of fact. "Kind of like that crossroad card, huh? But, for right now, I think you need to do as many normal things as possible. Otherwise, you'll obsess and go crazy. Distraction is good. Even though I would very much like to be that distraction and not this other guy."

Kevin laughed, gazing into Tyler's big blue eyes. "I really like this better version of you, Tyler. I really do."

"Me, too," the jock agreed, helping him into the passenger seat. "I like who I see in the mirror now."

Kevin masked his shudder with a warm smile as he slipped on his seatbelt. What he saw when he looked in the mirror terrified him because it was everything but normal starring back.

Tyler gently shut the door and walked around the front of his car and jumped into the driver seat, putting on his seatbelt. The engine roared to life, and he pulled out onto the road, switching gears as they went along. Lady Gaga's 'Dance in the Dark' was playing. Kevin reached over without much though and lightly rested his hand on top of Tyler's which was gripping the gearshift. The bigger blond looked over at him but didn't say anything.

"I could have really hurt you both," he whispered, gazing over at the jock. "Are you sure you're alright?"

Tyler took his eyes from the road for just a second and winked at him and gazed forward again. "You did not hurt me or Mrs Davenport."

He nodded his head and let out the heavy breath he had been holding in. That eased his mind a little.

"Your hand is cold," Tyler said. "Do you want me to turn the air off and roll the windows down?"

Kevin noticed he was holding Tyler's hand and almost pulled away but didn't. The bigger blond made no move to remove his hand either.

"No. Thanks. I'm good."

Tyler smiled over at him and turned his eyes back to the road in front of them. Kevin leaned his head back and closed his new eyes, listening to what he considered to be Lady Gaga's greatest song ever.

Chapter 31

Kevin's mind swirled with disbelief. Tyler Glace was in his bedroom sitting on his bed. The sight was so surreal that it seemed as though Tyler belonged there. Trying to comprehend the scene, Kevin shook his head before finally settling into the chair at his computer desk.

"Do you think your mom bought it?" Tyler asked, pushing himself back on the bed so he could sit cross legged.

Kevin shrugged his shoulders. "I don't know. Did you see the way she looked at me?"

Tyler nodded. "It looked like she had walked into a wall."

Kevin got up and went over to his dresser. He put his hand into a raku bowl he'd found in Roswell and pulled out a lighter and lit a candle that was surrounded by amethyst and citrine. He closed his eyes and stood there for a few moments until he could smell the familiar scent. Time for US to WAKE UP! He opened his eyes and shivered a little. That had been terrifying. He would never forget that nightmare smile. That infinite gaze. Those eyes could have flattened a mountain just by cocking a brow.

Glancing over his shoulder, he saw Tyler looking around his bedroom. "Is it what you were expecting?"

The jock's eyes followed him back to his chair.

"Yes. Just look at all these crystals. If you're not careful, you'll vibrate into a higher dimension."

Kevin blushed as he took his seat again. He had collected a lot of crystals from all the places he'd been. Some of them from out of the way shops and other's directly from nature. He only ever picked the ones which spoke to him.

"I recognize the Bast statue, but not sure who the image is carved in that stone relief over there," Tyler said, pointing.

"Inanna-Ishtar," Kevin answered him. "Mesopotamia. Lady of Heaven, Earth, and the Underworld."

Tyler nodded. "Nefertiti and…not a clue."

Kevin looked to see what he was looking at and grinned.

"That is either the Minoan Serpent Goddess or a high priestess in ritual garb. Some say she is Ariadne, Mistress of the Labyrinth. She helped Theseus defeat her brother, the Minotaur. He later abandoned her, and she married Dionysus, the god of wine and lavish parties."

Tyler glanced back at him.

"If not for the bed and computer desk, I'd say this room looked a bit like a temple." He pointed above Kevin's head. "Look at all the silks you have hanging from the ceiling and the different incense burners. And that's Freya. I recognize the feather robe. Wasn't she just as scary as Inanna?"

Kevin nodded. "When her anger rose one day, even Odin, the All Father fled his throne room in terror."

"Reminds me of someone I know," Tyler snorted.

Kevin rolled his eyes and gazed around his room and really took it all in. Crystals, candles, statues, sacred art hanging on the walls, objects that at one time had been sacred and worshipped for millennia. They were all replicas of museum pieces, of course. His bedroom always felt peaceful. He never felt scared when he was here, not even when he was left alone when his mom had to go away for seminars. When had he started collecting weird and ancient things? It must have been a little after his father had passed.

"Hey," Tyler said, bringing him back to the room. "Where'd you go?"

"Memories," Kevin answered him, sitting back in his chair. The other him flashed through his mind and it was like he could still feel that hand at his throat.

"Tyler?" He asked, sitting forward. "I need to share something with you, and it cannot leave this room."

The jock nodded his head. "It won't leave this room."

Kevin told him what he had seen when he'd been in the opaline room of his inner being. The taller blond scooted down to the floor so he could sit with his back against the foot of the bed and have his long legs stretched out in front of him so he could cross his ankles.

"That's...scary. This other 'you' wants to come out and it even used the royal US?"

Kevin then pointed at his new eyes. "I'm sure it has something to do with this."

Tyler was looking at him like he wanted to say something, but he wasn't. Kevin left the chair and got down on the floor to sit in front of the larger teen's bare feet.

"What?" Kevin asked. "You look like you want to say or ask something."

Tyler leaned forward. "Close the blind and curtains."

"Why?" Kevin asked.

"I want to see something," he told him.

Kevin got back to his feet and did as the jock asked. He twisted the blinds and pulled the curtains shut. He turned back around to Tyler and saw he breathed a sigh of relief.

"What?" Kevin asked.

"I was afraid they'd glow in the dark," Tyler told him.

Kevin cocked a brow and opened the curtains back up. He left the blinds closed because he liked the shadows the candlelight made dance along the walls.

"I'm glad they don't," Kevin said, walking back over to sit beside him. "I wouldn't know how to explain that."

"Struck by lightning?" Tyler asked.

Kevin snorted. "Is that how this works?"

The jock shrugged. He still couldn't believe Tyler Glace was in his bedroom. Never in a million years would he have thought this a possibility. The king jock and him were now friends.

"Kevin?" Tyler asked.

He turned his head to look at him. "Yeah?"

"I want to share something with you," he said, turning to stare at Kevin with those blue eyes. "But…I can't right now."

Kevin looked at him with concern.

"It's nothing bad," he said, giving Kevin a relieving smile. "At least I don't think it's anything bad. I just want to make sure it is what I think it is before I show you."

"Now you have me both curious and worried," Kevin told him. "I destroyed private property, and my eyes are now a completely differ-ent colour. What do you have to tell me?"

"I don't want to freak you out if I'm wrong," Tyler told him.

"Freak me out? Look who you're talking to," Kevin said. "Just tell me."

Tyler pulled his knee back and undid the ace wrap to reveal the bite wound he had seen in a photo was healed. It was like the bite had never been there. The skin was completely unmarred.

Kevin reached out and ran his finger over the unmarked skin and looked at him. "How?"

Tyler shrugged his shoulder and reached into his front pocket and pull out what appeared to be a switchblade. He then proceeded to slit his own palm before Kevin could react. Kevin yelped as a wave of warmth rushed over and through him like he'd suddenly stumbled into a sauna room. He quickly snatched hold of the jock's injured hand.

"Are you crazy?" He hissed, trying to keep his voice from getting above a concerned whisper. "What the hell, Tyler?"

"Watch," Tyler instructed, looking very curious at his bleeding palm.

Kevin looked up at him and then back down. His now violet eyes widened in awe.

"What the…?"

The jock's flesh began to slowly knit itself back together. The knife wound was closing before his eyes. The injured flesh lost that angry red look and flushed back to normal. Kevin carefully took his finger and wiped the blood away from where the cut had been just moments ago. The instant his flesh touched that blood, it was like a livewire jolted him. A man with hidden gifts.

"It's healed," Kevin whispered, gazing up at him. "That's amazing."

Tyler looked at him and his face was a mix of relief and shock.

"What?" Kevin asked.

"Your eyes are glowing," Tyler whispered.

Kevin jumped to his feet and raced over to his mirror. His eyes were glowing like a lantern had been lit within them. They reminded him of amethyst lamps. He could feel Tyler's blood on his finger, and he ever so slowly brought his finger up to look at it. It was like the blood had a song to it. It made the skin it touched hum a melody even sweeter. A force beyond him brought that bloody finger up to his mouth and rubbed his lips with it. As he watched, his lips began to glow red, and the skin around became illuminated. He felt Tyler's tall frame looming close behind him.

"What are you doing, Kev?"

Kevin looked at him in the mirror and licked his lips with a glowing tongue. "You taste like honey."

Tyler stepped closer. "You know that's how disease is spread right?"

"Are you diseased?" Kevin asked.

"No. I've had all my shots," the jock said.

Before Kevin could laugh, a sudden knock came at his bedroom door and both boys instantly panicked. Tyler quickly steered Kevin into the adjoined bathroom and closed the door after him.

"Everything all right in here?" Kevin heard his mother ask from the other side of the closed bathroom door.

"Kev needed the bathroom," he heard Tyler tell her. "Other than that, all good here. We were just discussing all the objects he's collected."

"I was wondering if you two were getting hungry," she said. "I was thinking about calling in some Mexican. You boys want to go pick it up? We can have dinner before Kevin's date arrives."

"Sounds like a plan," Tyler said. "I never turn down free food."

"I'll call it in now," she said, and Kevin heard the door close behind her.

A soft knock came at the door and Kevin opened it. Tyler stood just beyond the threshold.

"May I come in?"

Kevin stepped to the side and let him in.

Tyler walked by him and over to the sink. He began to open each drawer until he found a washcloth. He put it under the tap to wet it and rang it out. Walking over to where Kevin was leaning back against the wall, he put the rag to the smaller boy's lips and began to wipe his blood away.

Kevin allowed him to administer him. Tyler lifted his hand and began to wipe the blood from his glowing index finger.

"There," Tyler said, walking over to toss the cloth into the waste bin and hiding it under some tissue paper he pulled from the box. He turned back to Kevin and smiled. "The glow is starting to fade."

"What's happening to us?" Kevin whispered.

Tyler walked over and pulled him into his arms. "Secret gifts coming to light. At least we're not alone. We have each other to confide in."

Kevin allowed himself to be held. His heart was thundering in his chest, and yet Tyler's was steady as a drumbeat.

"What if Mrs Long did see a werewolf?" He asked.

"Shh," Tyler soothed, giving him a gentle squeeze, rubbing small circles along his back. "We're okay. Everything will be okay. Your mom is ordering Mexican and we're going to go pick it up."

"What are we going to do about this?" He asked.

"We'll figure it out," Tyler answered him. "Let's just focus on here and now. One moment at a time. We can't go back, only forward. We can plan."

Kevin furrowed his smooth brow. "When did you get so smart?"

"Always have been," the jock snorted. "And don't touch anymore blood. The last thing we need is for you to light up like a glowstick."

Kevin wrapped his arms around him. "Thank you for being my friend."

Tyler rested his chin on top of his head and held him like that until the smaller blonde's heart settled down.

"We're going to be fine," Kevin spoke after a few moments, not breaking contact. "Because we have each other's backs."

"Exactly," Tyler confirmed. "Partners."

"Partners," Kevin echoed.

"Ready to go pick up that Mexican?" Tyler asked.

Kevin slowly pulled away from him. "Am I normal?"

"Far from it," Tyler smiled, ruffling his hair. "And that's why I love you."

"You know what I mean," Kevin lightly chuckled, playfully punching his arm.

"Careful," Tyler teased, backing away, holding his arm. "You could break me."

Kevin glared at him. "You'll heal."

"Touché, Mr Rose," Tyler said, leading the way from the bathroom. "Now help me put my ace wrap back on, please. I don't want my parents asking questions."

Kevin got down on his knees and gently started to wrap the bandage back around the jock's ankle. He picked up the wrap clip and clipped it snuggly in place.

"Does it feel okay?" He asked, looking up at him. "Not too tight?"

Tyler smiled down at him. "It's perfect."

Tyler held out his hand and Kevin took it.

CHAPTER 32

After their laughter-filled dinner concluded, Kevin escorted Tyler to his car. The jock hugged him one final time before settling into the sleek confines of his Corvette and Genevieve sprang to life. He lowered the window and poked his head out, a captivating gaze fixated on Kevin's form. Time seemed to pause momentarily as their eyes locked in a wordless connection.

"Stop staring at them!" He whined, hiding his eyes behind his palms, peeking between his fingers.

"I'll text you every hour," Tyler said, giving him an assuring smile. His voice hummed through Kevin's every sinew like a vow. "Should you need me, I'll be there."

Kevin blinked his eyes and lowered his hands as a gentle wind stirred his locks. He nodded his head and gave the jock a smile back.

"See you tomorrow," Tyler said.

Kevin nodded. "See you tomorrow."

"I'll pick you up."

He waved Tyler off and waited for his taillights to vanish before going back inside.

"I can't believe that's the same boy you got into a fight with just a few days ago," his mother said, standing in the middle of the sitting room.

Kevin looked over at her. "I know."

"Are you sure you want to go on this date?" His mother asked, walking over to him.

He wasn't sure if he wanted to right now. Too much had happened in the span of one day.

"What do you mean?" He asked her.

She cocked her head to the side. "You really do have your blond moments. You'd have to be blind not to see the way that boy was looking at you all through dinner."

"I think you're reading too much into things," he told her.

She shook her head. "No subtitles required. His eyes were drinking you in, adoring you. A spark of worship even."

He stood there before her and looked down at his feet.

Her hand came up and touched his cheek. "Why are you wearing contact lenses?"

He didn't meet her gaze.

"Trying something new," he said, giving her a small smile. "Michael is taking me to see the remake of Fright Night. I thought I'd surprise him."

"Kids these days," she said, shaking her head. "Do you want me to check in on you?"

"Ty is."

His mom immediately gave him that all-knowing look. "Uh huh. I bet he even threatened to beat the guy up if he was to hurt you."

Kevin felt his cheeks start to burn.

"Okay," his mom said, turning away from him. She walked back over to take her seat on the sofa in front of the television. "Live and learn. We all have to."

He laughed. "Let me get dressed and you tell me what you think."

She waved him off.

Chapter 33

As she watched her son exit the room, she drew in a trembling breath, sensing her eyes welling up with emotion. Before she could regain control, tears streamed down her cheeks, silently cascading. She compelled herself to rise and seek solace in the kitchen, where she could conceal the sobs that shook her small frame.

Slowly making her way over to the counter, she dug through her purse for her cell. She saw she had three missed calls and five texts. Ignoring them, she made the call.

Putting the phone to her ear, she fought to keep her voice steady.

"Susan." A voice greeted her on the other end of the line.

"Naomi," she whispered. "It's happening."

"I know. We have much to discuss."

"I'll call you back when this boy comes to pick Kevin up. We must do something this time. I can't lose my son. I can't go through this again."

"At the moment, his true self is still bound. Give me time to put some counter measures in place. There are ways we can slow this down."

"This isn't chlamydia, Naomi!" She hissed, looking over her shoulder to make sure Kevin wasn't there listening. "There's no stopping this."

"Come to the shop when he's out."

The line went dead. Her cell slipped from her hand and landed on the tile facedown. She heard the screen crack, and she didn't even care. Taking a seat on the barstool, she had to stay calm and tell Kevin he looked good and not run and hold him. Things were happening to her son, and he was lying to her. She put a hand to her mouth. Did Tyler know? He either did, or her son was a very good actor. She had been lying to him as well. Lying about his father. It was true Kevin's father was no longer in this world. Kevin had witnessed that. It was just in the manner of how he exited it.

Alexander Rose, Kevin's father, did not leave this plane of existence due to a heart attack.

CHAPTER 34

Kevin posed before his floor-length mirror, admiring the ensemble he had carefully picked out. Clad in a sleek pair of form-fitting skinny jeans, he exuded confidence. The white t-shirt he wore boasted an artistically crafted infinity symbol, skilfully infused with vibrant hues of blue and purple, a masterpiece crafted by Sara. Completing his look were a pair of pristine white sneakers, his trusty silver watch, and the striking sterling silver Hand of Ishtar necklace that adorned his neck.

He gazed into his new violet eyes and turned his face from side to side, looking at them from different angles. They looked like normal eyes. Zero glow factor.

He blew out his Song of Angels candle, picked up the light jacket he'd gotten for free because he and his mom had toured a timeshare in Whistler last year. It tended to get cold in movie theatres and he wanted to be comfortable. He switched off his bedroom light and made his way down the steps. He could hear the television. His mom must have found something of interest to watch. She tended to channel surf because she hated commercials. He walked into the sitting room and stood there. She was wrapped up in a thin blanket and smiled when she looked over at him.

"Well?" He asked, posing for her. "How do I look?"

"Beautiful, Baby," she said, sitting up. "Just look at you."

He smiled. "You're saying that because you have to."

"No," she told him, shaking her head. "There are days you look like a chewed-up dog toy."

He gasped. "Take that back! I've never had a bad day."

She laughed. A knock came at the front door, and he spun around to look at it.

"He's here!"

His mom put her feet down on the floor. "Can I meet him?"

He nodded and slowly walked over to the door. He didn't want to appear too eager or excited to answer it. Such things seemed to be a turnoff for college aged guys. They didn't like clingy or needy. But too much indifference turned them off too. He had to walk that perfect balance between I want you inside me and I can live without you.

He reached out and opened the door, finding Michael standing there on his front porch in all his pale glory. That same handsome face with dark hair slicked back revealing a smooth brow. That smile on his devilish lips revealed those straight white teeth.

"Hello," Michael greeted with that deep voice of his. "You look nice. And those eyes are different. Cool."

"Thank you," Kevin said, words spilling from his mouth like he had practiced in front of the mirror. "We are seeing a vampire movie and I thought I'd cosplay a little. Would you like to come in for a few moments?"

Michael was gazing down at his chest. A subtle change flickered like a soft wave across that perfect face, almost too fast to catch, but Kevin had seen it. The look had bordered between annoyance and a little fear. He either hates my shirt or my necklace. Oh, God! Is it tacky? I thought it was subtle in its simplicity. But Tyler had liked it.

"Sure," Michael said.

Kevin opened the door wider. "Come on in."

Michael took the door and entered. Kevin led him into the sitting room where his mom was waiting.

"This is my mom," Kevin said. "She wanted to meet you."

Michael extended a hand to her. "It is very nice to meet you, Mrs Rose. I apologise for Kevin being late last time."

She shook his hand.

"It is nice to meet you also, Michael. You'll have my son home by eleven."

Kevin watched him nod his head.

"No mistake this time," Michael assured her. "He'll be home safe and sound before eleven. Promise."

She smiled at that.

"You both have a nice time and be safe. Look after him, Michael."

The older boy nodded his head. "He's perfectly safe with me."

"I'll follow you out," she said.

Kevin followed Michael out the door and onto the front porch. He looked towards the street to see a black Ferrari parked right in front of his home. He nearly tripped but caught himself before anybody could see his little stumble. Damn, he thought to himself. This guy's business must be very successful it he can afford a ride like that. Either that or his parents bought it for him.

"Buckle up!" His mom called after them.

He waved back to her as Michael opened the passenger side door for him. Instead of the door opening out, it opened straight up at an odd angle. He was not used to that. What if it falls and hits me?

"It's okay," Michael told him. "It won't fall."

He stepped within and took his seat. Michael closed the door after him. As Michael walked around to get in, he put his seatbelt on. The inside of the car smelled of sickening wealth. Michael put the key into the ignition and turned. The engine roared to life like a tiger about to pounce on prey.

"Ready?" The older boy looked over at him.

Kevin nodded and as they pulled out and took off, Michael honked the horn for his mother's benefit.

Damn! I forgot to get a photo of the license plate. DING! It was his mom. She had text him a photo of the license plate. He shook his head, chuckling to himself. He was his mother's son. He looked over at Michael and smiled before sending the photo to Tyler.

A wolf howled. He had changed Tyler's text tone again.

Tyler (the sorry jock) Glace: *If you don't answer any of my texts within three minutes, I'm calling the police. Be mindful!* He grinned.

Beautiful Boy: *Thank you! Talk soon!*

"I already have the movie tickets," Michael said, speeding up a little in a 55 zone. "Our seats are at the very back and they recline."

Kevin looked over at him. "You're taking me to the fancy theatre?"

Michael nodded, flashing him a sharp grin. "Only the best. You can order whatever you want off the menu, too."

Kevin smiled. "Welcome to Fight Night."

Michael sped up. "For real."

Chapter 35

Kevin was left speechless as they arrived at the Blue Grotto Multiplex, marvelling at the vast expanse of emptiness that stretched before them. The parking lot, scarcely occupied, had no more than twenty vehicles. Although it was a Sunday night and tomorrow was a workday, Kevin couldn't help but be taken aback by how empty the place looked.

Summer vacation was just beginning. Where was everyone? Something strange was happening and he didn't know what. Michael pulled into a parking spot near the front, but away from the other cars and Kevin didn't blame him. One had to park just far enough away, but also where security cameras could see. This was the kind of car that just begged to be keyed by jealous eyes.

"Take your ticket and go get your seat," Michael told him, handing it across to him. "And I will meet you shortly. I've got to make a quick call. One of my clients is being difficult. I felt my phone vibrate all the way here."

Kevin took the ticket and gave him a grin. "See you in there then."

The dark headed teen nodded and pulled out his phone.

CHAPTER 36

The child of the night held his mobile phone to his ear, observ-ing his meal as it ventured into the movie theatre. He knew he would soon follow suit. The illuminated doors and windows reflected in the vibrant lights, and he couldn't afford the risk of the mortal noticing his lack of reflection. Glancing into the rear-view mirror, he confronted the empty void staring back at him and swiftly adjusted it to its proper position. He mentally noted to remain cautious of the troublesome silver watch and the accursed holy symbol adorning the innocent throat.

After a brief pause, he exited the vehicle that had transported him and his most recent sustenance. With a press of the lock button, he fulfilled the customary practice and ventured inside to locate his intended meal. The task would prove effortless. With his last meal's American Express Black Card, he had secured exclusive occupancy of every seat in the room. They would not be interrupted. Should the meal prove satisfying, tonight could mark the transformation into a vampire, granting it the status of a real boy.

CHAPTER 37

The older teenager's statement about their seats being at the back of the room was far from a joke. Their seating arrangement was positioned right at the rear, elevated on a separate level. It was like having their very own exclusive viewing balcony, with the rest of the seats positioned below them.

Some 80's retro remix of Ava Max's 'Sweet but Psycho' was playing over the speakers. Probably to get viewers in the mood to see a remake of a beloved 80's cult classic.

He took a seat in his chair, and it was incredibly comfortable.

There was a button on the armrest, and he pushed it. The chair began to unfold and down he went. This is sweet!

"How is it?" A voice asked, looming over the back of his seat.

Kevin yelped and the older boy laughed as he walked around to take his seat beside him.

"I'm sorry," Michael apologised, slipping his cell into his pocket. "Some people have no concept of professional boundaries."

Kevin glared over at him. "I've had better."

Michael cocked a dark brow. "Really?"

Kevin nodded. "Yes."

"Hmm," Michael contemplated, moving to get up. "If this isn't good enough for you…"

Kevin reached out and grabbed his arm laughing. "It's perfect!"

He said, pulling on the handsome boy's strong arm. "Look how private it is. I bet you paid quite a bit for these seats."

Michael shrugged his shoulders. "I like having a good time in comfortable surroundings," he said, pushing the button on his armrest, having his chair lay back.

Kevin pulled a menu out of the slot on the side of his chair and opened it up. They served everything from burgers to grilled cheese sandwiches. He wasn't really all that hungry. He'd had a lot of tacos with his mom and Tyler. Tyler… His heart did a funny little pitter patter, and he looked over at Michael. The guy was very good looking, and he was kind…but…

"I actually think we might have this whole room to ourselves," the older boy said, smiling over at him. "The movie starts in a few minutes."

"It's weird," Kevin said, gazing around the empty room. "Where is everyone?"

"It is summer," Michael answered, following his gaze. "Vacations?"

Kevin bit his bottom lip and slowly nodded his head. "It's possible, but the place is starting to crawl with tourists. Why aren't they here?"

Michael chuckled. "When I vacation, I never go to the movies."

Kevin was about to object, but then thought better of it. "Come to think of it, I never go to the movies when Mom and I travel."

Michael nodded his head. "See? Now, how about we order something before the lights go off?"

Kevin lifted his menu back up and settled on a grilled chicken wing box smothered in hot sauce with a Mountain Dew.

"Is that all?" Michael asked. "No wonder you're so small."

"Did you just call me skinny?" Kevin glared.

Michael slowly nodded his head.

That glare turned into a smile. "You're sweet."
Michael snorted.

CHAPTER 38

Kevin's body jolted in surprise as Charley Brewster's mother swung the sharp wooden end of her realtor sign down, piercing through Jerry Dandrige's back. In response, the vampire let out an ear-piercing shriek, his voice reaching unnaturally high pitches as if possessed by demonic Regan MacNeil herself. Desperately, he writhed in agony, attempting to extract the impaling object. In that moment, Kevin's gaze shifted to Michael, who nonchalantly tossed handfuls of popcorn into his mouth. Their eyes met, and Michael's gaze, filled with a captivating coolness, locked onto Kevin. The older boy flashed a mischievous grin before returning his attention to the scenes unfolding on the screen ahead.

He suddenly felt his cell vibrate and pulled it from his pocket. He had his night screen on. It was Tyler.

Tyler (the sorry jock) Glace: *Just checking on you.*

He smiled in the dark and typed back.

Beautiful Boy: *All good. Thank you. The movie is okay. No dance scene or romantic seductions. Talk soon.*

He slipped his phone back into his pocket. He looked to see Michael gazing at him. Those eyes were once again beginning to pull him in. It felt as though he was falling into them.

Michael lifted his armrest between them and pat the area for Kevin to move closer to him. Kevin felt as though he couldn't resist that subtle invitation. A hand gently took him by the arm and began to pull him in.

Kevin soon found Michael was on top of him. A sexy weight pressing down on him and those steel eyes sucking him in deeper. The smell of the older boy was making him fuzzy brained. Those red lips were on his and that tongue was teasing his own. The more he breathed the more delicious Michael smelled. It was like all he was breathing was the older boy. Those brutal lips and tongue traced along his throat. Sucking and licking at his skin. Michael pressed his hips down against him, and Kevin could feel the older teen was turned on.

His eyes opened wide, when he felt a slight sting in his throat that began to grow into something more. His mouth opened wide, and he felt like his whole body had been submerged in a jacuzzi and all the jets were hitting him at once.   It wasn't unpleasant.

Both his hands grabbed roughly at Michael's hair, gripping with a strength that must have surprised the older boy, causing that mouth to disconnect. Kevin lifted that face to meet his own and he could see his violet eyes reflecting with a glow in Michael's.

"Worship USsssssssssssssssss," he hissed, pressing Michael's face into his neck with a strength he never had before.

He could feel something deep down within him ascending and the closer it got to the surface the less human he felt. He started to feel completely other. Wild. Free. In your face and just out of reach. Unknowable. Untouchable.

The older teen struggled against him and broke free, rolling away from him. Michael was all shadows and mist. Kevin felt his body sit up with fluid grace that no human possessed and the voice that came from his lips was older, deeper, a growl that was all honeysuckle and razor wire. "What'ssssss the matter, Mikey? Don't you want USssssss anymore?"

That laugh was smoke before a blaze… and then Kevin was suddenly in control of his faculties again. Kevin froze when he saw what was standing back, looming just beyond him. If he had ever needed to make his mind up about a guy, it sure as hell was made up now.

What stood there in the flickering shadows was terrifying.

"What are you?" Michael snarled at him.

His voice was old and as distorted as his face. His eyes were glowing red embers that had been left to slowly die in a forgotten fireplace. Those big hands had fingers that were long and ended in curved nails that looked like hooks. His back was bent and deformed.

"I can taste it in your blood. It's different now. You're not human!"

Not human. I'm not human? Then what the heck are you?

Kevin touched his neck and felt warmth under his fingers. Pulling his hand away he gazed at what should have been red blood on his hand. He blinked several times at his fingers. The residue was shimmering gold against the glow of his skin.   The older boy crouched, and Kevin quickly looked at him. Those already abnormally long fingers grew into even longer black talons and Michael hissed at him with a mouth full of monstrous teeth.

That once handsome face was disfigured and grotesque.

"I will not ask again! What are you?"

"What am I?" Kevin asked, rising on shaking legs. "What are you?"

Michael hissed at him with a forked tongue slithering between shark thin lips. "Vampire."

The snake with the scythe over its head…

"Oh, this is fantastic!" Kevin crazy laughed, slowly trying to back away to put as much space between him and fang boy. "A vampire taking a young boy to a vampire flick and not even an original one! It could have at least been Bram Stoker. Oh. My. God. Just how old are you anyway?"

He narrowed his eyes, feeling sick and pointed at him in anger. "You paedophile!"

"Shut up!" Michael shrieked, looking like he was struggling to regain a more human form. "Just shut up!"

Kevin's mind was reeling. I kissed that? I made out with this! Freya, Isis, Astarte! Rage! Michael's visage kept flickering between young and decrepit; monstrous and beautiful. He couldn't seem to hold onto a single form.

"Wait. What did you just say to me?" Kevin asked, looking for a way to get past Michael, feeling all the blood beginning to rise to his head. "Who do you think you are? You might be a vampire. You might even be hot when you don't look like a dried-out hunchbacked elephant scrotum, but I will not be spoken to like that, Sir! I have a 3.8 GPA! I got a near perfect score on the SAT! I've been accepted to Mainland University! And I can tear a building apart because there is something scary inside of me AND I DON'T KNOW WHAT THE FUCK IT IS!"

The ground beneath Kevin's feet trembled and fractured, heading straight toward the startled vampire. Michael, in response, emitted a fierce growl in the face of the approaching shockwave. With a remarkable display of defiance against gravity, he leaped into the air and remained suspended, seemingly weightless. The sight was reminiscent of an intimidating red balloon, but with an unnaturally wide mouth brimming with needle-like teeth and talons so sharp they could effortlessly slice through metal.

The air in the room became Arctic cold, and Kevin could see his own breath. His hands began to glow even brighter. His skin glimmered like magnesium about to ignite.

Let Us out, a voice louder than the one that was always present in his head thundered over a mountain of rushing water.

"And here I was going to grant you the gift of eternity," Michael spoke and his voice was hollow as a tomb. "Now I am going to rip your skinny carcass to pieces!"

At least the demon still thinks I'm skinny.

Michael launched himself at him, and Kevin screamed at the top of his lungs, putting his glowing hands up to defend himself. The predator landed on top of him, causing him to fall back onto the ground with a crash. The vampire had hold of his wrists, squeezing them to the point where Kevin's screams became even higher causing the air around them to vibrate, but suddenly Michael's flesh began to sizzle and pop, smoking like a sparkler. The vampire roared and let out an ear-piercing shriek and leaped off him with a crocodile snarl.

Kevin rolled over onto his side to watch Michael fly and jump from the balcony. He quickly got to his feet and saw Michael racing down the rows of empty seats with white hot flames spreading up both of his arms. The vampire literally ran right through the exit door with a metal tearing BAM.

Kevin took a slight step back and fell into his reclined chair. Tears streaming down his face. He looked at his hands and arms. The white-hot glow was blinding, but it was also beginning to subside. *What's happening to me?* He sat there for a few moments and with shaking hands, watched the light fade. When he was sure he wasn't going to set his clothes on fire, he reached into his pocket and pulled out his phone. He brought up Tyler and called. It only rang the once.

"Hi! How was it?"

"Ty..." His voice was shaking. He could barely hold the phone.

"What's wrong? You sound weird. Are you okay?"

"Will you come get me...please?" He burst out crying. "He attacked me... and ran away..."

"Get somewhere safe! Find someone. A crowd. I'm on my way."

The jock wasted no time asking questions.

"Okay," Kevin said, quickly making his way down the stairs and peeking around the door before quietly stepping out. Another 80's retro remix was playing. It sounded a lot like Rihana's 'Disturbia' echoing through the long empty hall. The lights were dim and the whole place felt terrifying now. He took off at a run towards the lobby only to stop in his tracks when he got there. It was too quiet. Why was it so quiet? Where was everyone? He looked over to the left and saw something slumped back against the side of a cardboard movie display.

"Kevin?" Tyler asked in his ear. "Kevin? Talk to me. I'm in my car now."

His blurry eyes began to focus through the unshed tears.

"Kevin?"

"I think someone might be hurt," he whispered, breaking out into goosebumps and shivering. "They're on the ground. I think I see blood."

"Don't go outside. He could be out there waiting. Hide somewhere!" Tyler demanded.

Is she dead?

"Kevin!"

"Okay," he whispered, quickly ducking into the men's restroom as quietly as he could.

He didn't run to the last stall, but to the middle one. They always went to the last stall in the movies. He ran in and pushed the door as closed as he could, without locking it. He didn't want the red in use sign to be seen.

"I'm in the men's restroom," he whispered, sitting with both feet on the toilet seat so he couldn't be seen should someone look under the slightly raised plastic walls. "Please hurry."

"Stay on the line," Tyler told him. "I'm calling 911. Hang on."

Kevin struggled to calm his breathing, while he was on hold. He kept taking deep breaths in through his nose and releasing them through his mouth in slow exhales. Fantasy was no longer make-believe anymore. Truth was a thing far stranger than any fiction. He had just set a vampire ablaze and damaged another room.

It was eerie quiet. He wished Tyler would hurry up and come back on the line. He was getting more afraid. The phone beeped in his ear and Tyler was suddenly talking to him again.

"I'm right here. I'm almost there. Just be quiet. Make no sounds. The police are literally right next door at the doughnut shop."

He could hear the growl of Tyler's engine.

"He's a vampire," Kevin whispered. "Fangs, claws, he can fly. I think I hurt him though. I split the floor apart. I bleed gold now. I glow like a firework. He ran away."

He just kept talking because he felt like he was losing his mind.

"You're bleeding?" Tyler asked. "Did he hit you?"

The engine got even louder. He could hear Tyler shifting gears. He must have been going a hundred.

"Get something to stop the bleeding," Tyler demanded. "Quietly and quickly."

He carefully unrolled some toilet paper and put it to his neck. He could hear sirens.

"I can hear the police."

"I'm about a minute away. Stay where you are until the police find you. They've had sugar. I don't need you accidentally getting shot."

Memories at the beach. The wind. The water. The moon so high over his head. The dunes in the distance.

"Ty," Kevin whispered, tears starting to choke him again. "I'm really scared. He jumped on me. He bit me. I think he's bitten me before. Is…is this why I am the way I am?"

"It's going to be okay," Tyler tried to soothe him. "Just try and stay as calm as you can. You're hidden. You said he ran away. He must be long gone by now."

"He ran away on fire through a metal door," Kevin sobbed. "But yeah…the sirens should deter him."

He squeaked when he heard the bathroom door open.

"Police! Anyone in here? Kevin?"

It was a voice he thought he recognized.

"Hello? This is Officer Davidson. You're safe now."

"Here!" He called out. "I'm back here."

"I just parked," Tyler said in his ear. "Running up to the cops now."

"Okay," Kevin said, dropping his phone back into his pocket.

Kevin got down and dropped the bloody tissue in the toilet before slowly walking out of the stall and towards the officer. She put her gun away.

"Oh, Kevin," the female officer said, taking him by the arms. "Sweetie, it's Linda. I go to your mom's office. She cleans my daughter's teeth."

She led him out of the restroom, and the girl he'd found by the display was sitting up with another officer. She looked as if she was coming out of a daze.

"Yeah," he said, too shaken to listen to what was being said to him.

"Kevin!" Tyler yelled, taking his already fragile attention away from her.

He saw Tyler and took off running towards him, and literally jumped into his arms. That big strong embrace enfolded him, and he started crying all over again.

"Davidson!" Another officer shouted over his sobs. "We got a few more unconscious people over here behind the counters."

CHAPTER 39

Michael's contorted form resembled a gnarled tree branch, distorted by the fury of an unforgiving tempest. His weathered countenance drooped, revealing sagging jowls, as he gazed in horror at his hands. Charred to the core, they remained trapped in a state of unyielding decay, defying the natural course of his healing powers. An inferno raged within him, consuming every fibre of his being. It was as though the boy's very blood, infused with divine essence, was tearing him asunder, akin to the effect of consuming blessed water.

Collapsing against a weathered brick wall, Michael lifted his gaze towards the night sky. His flesh had been set ablaze by the mere touch of the boy. He still felt the relentless onslaught of invisible, scorching white flames, mercilessly licking away at his existence.

Those eyes. Never have I seen anything like those eyes before. In his 60 years of life, never had he felt such agonizing pain. Nothing had ever damaged him like this. Not even sunlight. WHAT IS HE?

Fear. He felt absolute fear. And HATE. A deep seething hatred overtook him.   Never had he felt such hate towards someone.

An opening door caught his attention, and he glared through slits from the shadows with eyes of a viper, seeing flickers of orange and red radiating heat from a warm body. I must drink. I must heal myself.

"Hey, Dude!" A male voice called from the open doorway to what must have been the back of a restaurant. A long-haired man who looked a bit like a surfer stepped out to berate him. "You can't be back here."

Faster than darkness, Michael slithered from the shadows stretched and elongated by pain and snatched the guy by his arm and dragged him from the light before he could make a sound of distress. He sank a mouthful of sharp teeth into that throat and tore. Warmth flooded his mouth, and he drank as the human writhed in his desiccated arms.

When he sated his thirst, he tossed the twitching body over into the dumpster, slamming the lid down hard. A sharp cramp ripped through his stomach, and he hunched over and violently vomitted. He thought by drinking fresh blood, it was going to help him heal, but it was doing the opposite. Blood and thick black ooze sprayed from his gaping maws as he went down on his knees, clutching at his throat with his badly burned talons. Son of a bitch! What has he done to me? He began to crawl with great difficulty back into the gathering shadows. Drinking blood was not helping.

He held his trembling hands out in front of him. They were smoking and crumbling away to ash before his horrified eyes. No! My beautiful body! He's destroyed my beautiful body! He hissed and snarled as pain once again ripped with fire through his gut. He bent over and vomited a gory scream onto the concrete.

Throwing his head back and arching his spine, he screamed as his fingers started to disintegrate, then his hands, his wrists, his arms. He saw those violet eyes glowing down at him and his whole body collapsed under the weight of their awesome gravity.

No more noise came from his mouth as he crumbled away in a breeze, leaving behind only his clothes and the bloody mess that would be burned away in the morning light.

The vampire that called himself Michael was no more, but his demise had been felt thousands of miles away by the one who had made him all those decades ago. That terrible cry rose from an abyss on the wings of a million infernal terrors.

Chapter 40

Officer Davidson was just about done recording Kevin's statement when his attention was captivated by the sight of his mother arriving at the multiplex in her car. In an instant, he rose from his seat with Tyler, overcome with anticipation, as Mrs Davenport emerged from the passenger side.

"What happened?" His mother yelled, running up to where they were at the back of an ambulance, wrapping her arms around him. "Are you okay?"

"Hello, Susan," Officer Davidson greeted her.

"Linda," Kevin's mom said, looking her son over, and then looking at the officer. "What's happened?"

"Your son states he has been assaulted by his date," Officer Davidson informed her, holding a clipboard. "My partner and a few other officers are combing the Ferrari."

Kevin saw his mother's face begin to crack.

"What did he do to you?" She asked, looking at him, pulling him in closer. "Did he touch you? Did he put his hands on you?" She looked around. "Where is he?"

"Gone," Kevin whispered, reaching back to take hold of Tyler's hand again. "I put up a fight and he didn't like that."

"What's with all these ambulances?" Mrs Davenport asked, coming up.

"Others have been injured by something," Officer Davidson stated. "We're not sure what's happened but we are assessing everything."

"Officer Davidson," a voice came across on her radio.

She brought her radio up. "Go ahead."

"I'm filtering through the security feed and nobody fitting the victim's description of his assailant is on the video. There are a few seconds here where the automatic doors open, but nobody comes in. You also need to see this. Something very strange. The workers behind the counter all seem to freeze for a moment and then one by one hit the ground. Possible gas leak maybe?"

Kevin went cold. Officer Davidson looked at him.

"What is he then? Invisible? That's impossible." Kevin's mother snapped. "I saw him, Linda. He came into my home. My son sure as hell did not drive a Ferrari here by himself. He doesn't even know how to drive a manual. Just look at him. He's shaking."

The ticket seller who had been at the door came walking around with the help of another officer at her side.

"This beautiful dark headed man said he needed some help and the last thing I remember is waking up with you over me. Did he leave me his number at least?"

"See!" Kevin's mom said, pointing. "Even she saw him."

"Take your son home, Susan," Officer Davison directed her. "I'll be in touch later. Nothing like this has ever happened here before. I'm just glad nobody has been seriously injured."

His mother put her hand on his shoulder. He let his mother steer him away with Mrs Davenport on his other side. Tyler followed along behind.

"I'll ride with Tyler," he said, stopping short that it almost caused the taller blond to walk right into him.

"Sweetie, I need to…"

"Take him to the shop," Mrs Davenport said matter of fact. She was looking at him with an intense gaze. "He has to know the truth, and he has to tell us what really happened in there."

"Truth?" Kevin asked. "What truth?"

"Shop," Mrs Davenport repeated herself. "Now."

His mom looked from him to Tyler. She took his hand in hers.

"You've really been here for Kevin," she said, squeezing his hand tight. "Thank you."

Tyler nodded. "Of course."

"What truth?" Kevin asked again.

"Come on, Susan," Mrs Davenport said, holding out her hand to usher her along. "I'll take us, Dear. You drive like a maniac."

"We'll follow you," Tyler told them.

Kevin was glaring daggers but allowed him to put an arm around him and they both made their way over to his Corvette. He opened the door for Kevin and the smaller blond got in. He watched Tyler run around the front and jump into the driver's seat beside him.

"What truth?" He whispered. "I'm scared."

Tyler reached for him and pulled him into a hug.

"Michael is a vampire, Tyler," he said, squeezing his eyes shut, letting himself be held. "He bit me. He took my blood. And then I split the floor and lit up like a matchstick."

Tyler held him while he kept talking.

"I was bleeding, and my blood was gold," he went on. "I'm completely healed though. I had to play it off as party paint. I managed to get most of it off me, but it has stained by shirt. How did I heal so fast?"

Tyler reached up and turned the overhead light on.

Kevin showed him his shirt. It was stained golden.

Tyler blinked and then looked into his violet eyes. "I believe you, Kev."

HONK! Both boys jumped.

Dammit, Mom!

Mrs Davenport gestured, and Tyler started the car. Florence +

the Machine's 'Cosmic Love' was playing as the jock followed along behind the local witch and Kevin's mom.

Kevin felt Tyler take hold of his hand and squeeze it before letting go to shift Genevieve into a higher gear. Kevin put his head back against the seat and gazed out the window, blowing a loose lock out of his face.

"And this shirt is one of a kind. Jesus Christ!"

Tyler snorted and reached to hold his hand again as they cruised along after the car in front of them.

CHAPTER 41

Mrs Davenport swiftly guided the trio into her shop, gently closing the door behind them. As Kevin stepped inside, a distinct click echoed, signalling the secure locking of the door. In a hushed tone, she whispered a mystical incantation, her index finger tracing a symbol on the glass. With his newfound perception, Kevin's eyes discerned the radiant emblem taking shape—an exquisite alteration of the Venus symbol, adorned with a captivating eight-pointed star at the crown of the cross. The Morning Star. Queen of Heaven and Earth. *How am I able to see this?*

"I would like for you all to take a seat in the Reading Room," she told them, lighting the candles that were situated all around the altar of the faceless goddess.

Kevin trailed behind his mother, with Tyler hot on his heels, the jock faithfully by his side. The taller blond was like his shadow. As Kevin glanced towards the closed-off Reiki Room he had previously reduced to ruins, a tinge of remorse washed over him.

"Tyler?" Kevin's mom asked. "Do your parents know where you are?"

Tyler cracked a sly grin and scratched the back of his head. "You do know my dad is a doctor and my mom's a nurse. They are both on-call twenty-four-seven."

Kevin's mother cocked a sculpted brow at him. Tyler pulled out his cell phone. "I'll send them a quick text and let them know where I am."

"Okay!" Kevin rolled his eyes. "Can someone please tell me what this TRUTH thing is already. Too much is happening all at once and I really do feel like I'm about to snap."

"Well, we certainly can't have you snapping," Mrs Davenport said, stepping into the reading room. The assorted rainbow beads swishing and clacking in her wake. "You've already destroyed one room today."

"And Cinema Room Three," Kevin added. "Split the balcony apart and set my date on fire."

His mother looked at him with wide eyes. "Oh, god."

"God. Indeed." Mrs Davenport said, taking a seat across from the smaller blond. "Please tell us what happened tonight."

Kevin took a deep breath in and let it out slowly between his teeth. He started by telling them how Michael was a vampire. A big scary vampire that tried to eat him.

"He took me to see a remake of this 80's vampire flick, which, I only recommend if you haven't seen the original. And…I'm actually really offended."

Mrs Davenport cleared her throat. Tyler reached over and gently held his hand.

"Mouth full of fangs. Fingers that were too long and ended in sharp claws. He can fly and he's super strong. He bit me. I think he bit me twice actually. On the beach would have been the first time. Did I mention I bleed gold now?"

He showed them the stains he had on his ruined shirt. He just knew Sara was going to throw something at him.

"I began to glow from the inside out, he jumped me, and he went up like it was the Fourth of July in Texas."

"And he ran away?" His mother asked.

"On fire," he nodded. "On white hot fire."

His mother paled. "Naomi?"

Mrs Davenport was squeezing the bridge of her nose. "You need to tell him what really happened to his father, Susan."

His mother met his gaze and her bottom lip quivered as tears began to fill her eyes.

"Your father," she said, closing her eyes and taking in a shaky breath. "Your father was an avatar. It happened a little before he also turned eighteen."

Kevin blinked. "My dad was a Nickelodeon cartoon?"

"Your dad was…is a God," Mrs Davenport corrected him matter of fact. "A deity on earth. Divine. Holy. Sacred. Revered. Feared."

"My dad is dead," Kevin said, shaking his head. "I saw him die."

"No," his mom gently said to him. "He didn't die. You only saw what he left behind. A shell."

"A mortal shell can't hold the divine for very long," Mrs Davenport said. "It burns out. The vessel tends to expire at an early age when the divine within fully awakens."

LET US OUT!

"Your father was lucky," his mother continued, looking like she was really struggling to keep back the flow of tears beginning to take form in her eyes. "He almost made it to 40."

"And at the rate you're going," Mrs Davenport snapped. "You'll be lucky if you make it to twenty."

His eyes widened. Tyler growled under his breath.

"Naomi!" His mother hissed at her, and then looked back at him. "She doesn't mean that."

"That clearing did this to him," Tyler said, rising to his feet. He looked really upset. "If we had never done that. If you…" The taller blond was glaring at Mrs Davenport and Kevin could see the whites of his eyes filling with blood. "You knew this would happen to him."

"This was destined to happen regardless," Mrs Davenport stated matter of fact. "When the body matures to the right conditions, the divinity reborn within begins to stir. If not here in my shop where it was somewhat contained, Kevin could have severely injured or killed hundreds, including you. And he would have been exposed. Hell. Our world may already be exposed due to that stupid vampire and that goddamn werewolf pissing in that silly woman's birdbath."

Werewolf...?

"Koi pond!" Tyler snapped and then his mouth gaped for but a second.

Kevin reached out for him and took hold of his shaking hand. The taller blond looked like he wanted to punch something and argue some more, but he took his seat next to Kevin and let his hand be held.

"Sweetheart," his mother said, scooting forward in her chair. "I'm so sorry to have kept this from you, all I can do is apologise."

I'm a God. He closed his eyes.

"Is that with a big G or a little g?" he asked.

"I really don't think that matters in the slightest," Mrs Davenport said.

He looked up at her and her eyes met his violet gaze.

"I can teach you how to mostly stay in control of your emotions. It helped your father. Learning to keep some form of control will help you not burn through your vessel so fast." Mrs Davenport told him.

"But, when the divine finally does take hold," his mother said. "When all your memories return, no amount of meditation, mantras, or chanting is going to matter. You just are. It is hard for a God to remain in this dense matter. Your vibration will not be compatible for this dimension. The possibility of Armageddon is very high."

"You are going to become a magnet. A star in the centre of a galaxy," Mrs Davenport went on. "All manner of people will be drawn to you. They'll tell you their sins and all their secrets. They'll even want you to punish them. And they will want to love you. Desire you. They will offer you everything."

Kevin's mind immediately went to Galadriel's monologue when

Frodo willingly offered her the one ring to rule them all.

"So, you're saying I should start a cult?" he asked.

His mother snorted. "Your dad said that, but we had to keep him hidden, cloaked. If those who are in the know knew a God was among them, they would have killed him. Just by leaving this dimension for another could tear this universe apart. Luckily, your father's ascension had been peaceful."

"Is that why dad devoted his practice to charity work?" He asked her. Certain things clicking into place and memories made more sense now.

His mom nodded.

"Another reason why he lasted as long as he did here in this dimension. People worshipped him without knowing it and he took their donations as offerings. He helped build a lot of homes and schools in other countries." She told him.

Kevin looked down at the large hand holding his. He gazed back up into Tyler's brilliant blue eyes. Now I understand. He can't help himself. He adores me. Tyler shook his head as if he was reading Kevin's mind.

"I loved you before all of this happened. Remember that."

Love. He loves me. Tyler Glace loves me. He says he loves me!

"I'm never growing old because I'll never make it that far…"

"No, Kevin," Mrs Davenport leaned towards him reassuringly. "The memories of who and what you are will surface in time. You will never die. You can't die. You bleed divine ichor now. You'll step from your shell like throwing off a shirt. It's not the same as one of us. You will ascend back to your plane. Your divine realm. Olympus. Asgard. Heaven. Whatever it is you call it. It could be an entire universe of your own design. What you are wearing now, is but a costume to remove. And hopefully, when you do cast your shell off, you won't destroy the world in the process."

"That doesn't make any of this any easier, Naomi," his mother said, looking at him with those big eyes. "If the world survives, I'll be left here. Tyler will be left here."

I could destroy the world. Tyler squeezed his hand. I could hurt my mom. I could hurt...Tyler... Kevin wanted to comfort them, but he didn't know how. Not yet. He looked at his mom and Mrs Davenport.

"What about Michael? He's still out there somewhere. What if he comes back?"

He paled.

"I invited him into our home..."

"That is a problem," Mrs Davenport nodded, sitting back. "And it is one I can easily solve by casting a spell to keep him out, but I seriously doubt he will ever come near you again. When a vampire gets burned, they stay away, and you burned him with pure divinity. Your divine ichor is probably burning through him as we speak. It will take years for him to heal completely, if at all. Depending on how much he drank, he may be a pile of ash blowing about in the breeze this very moment."

"But he's going to hurt people," Kevin said. "He's probably hurting people right now trying to heal himself."

Mrs Davenport nodded. "That's what vampires do, but he has his own predators."

"And those are?" Tyler asked.

"Hunters," she answered him. "Werewolves, and those rare few Gods born into flesh for some crime to learn a lesson."

Crime? Lesson? What the fuck did I do? His ass vibrated and he jumped up with a yelp. His cell phone was vibrating in his back pocket. Michael?

Reaching into his pocket with a shaky hand, he pulled it out, and glanced at the screen with dread. It was Sara! Oh, thank god... me!

Sara: *My cousin just told me something crazy went down at the Multiplex. She said she saw you there with Tyler. Are you okay? What happened? Some terrorist gas attack?*

He quickly sent her a message back.

Kev: *All good here. Safe and sound. Talk soon! Hugs! Kisses!*

While his mom and Mrs Davenport talked, he quickly found Michael's number and blocked it. He was going to have to change his number anyway.

"I will follow you both home and perform the necessary spell to revoke a vampire's invitation, and I will need Kevin's help as well." Mrs Davenport said.

"My help?" he asked.

She nodded. He looked at Tyler.

"Will you stay the night? I really don't want to be alone right now."

The smile he received from the jock was beautiful.

"I'll send my parents another text," Tyler said, reaching for his mobile.

He leaned over and rested his head against the jock's bare shoulder.

CHAPTER 42

The warm glow of the honeybee Tiffany lamp bathed Kevin's bedroom in a delicate, stained-glass light, casting patterns that danced along the trails of incense meandering through the air. With a gentle crawl onto his bed, Kevin nestled his head onto a pillow infused with the soothing aroma of jasmine. Observing Tyler leisurely removing his black Gucci pool sliders, he joined Kevin on the bed, enveloping him with a muscular arm and pulling him close against his larger frame. A rush of warm breath playfully caressed Kevin's neck, eliciting a smile from within. Night by Zola Jesus was softly playing from his desktop.

Mrs Davenport had revoked Michael's invitation with a ritual and by having Kevin say, nothing unholy may entire this home for a God resides within. This was because, she said, when a God speaks, all will listen, and all may choose to obey or be smitten. There is always a choice. Submit, be utterly devoured, or strike a bargain. I am never going to be like that. I will do things myself.

He could smell the bigger teen's cologne. Lemon and cedar. His eyes followed the amber trail of incense smoke as it snaked its way through the air towards where they both lay. It smelled so much better than how he remembered. The sticks were handmade by Mrs Davenport from juniper and cedarwood and the smoke somehow smelled sweeter than ever before.

Prayer. It was the scent of delicious prayer. It was the scent of Tyler's prayer. Tyler had lit the incense stick and placed it upright in the bronze burner. The jock had stood there for a few moments gazing at the smoke as it rose into the air.

Kevin closed his eyes and breathed in the sweet smoke and Tyler's secret prayer filled his ears like song being carried on soft feathers. *I don't really pray a lot, and I don't think any of them have ever been answered. I'm not knocking you or any of you…but…I really like this guy… and I want him…and he needs to stay here because I have a lot to make up for and I need to make what time he does have here better. I don't want him to ever leave. So, I'll make him happy. I'll make him feel loved. I'll try my best not to hurt him or make him cry. In fact, I will do so much better than try because I don't think I can heal from a lightning smite. I did accidentally stick my finger in a light socket the other day, but that just gave me a slight buzz. You get the point! I want him to stay. I'll light candles. I'll burn incense. I'll work hard and build him a temple worthy of his worship. Just let him stay. I need him to stay.*

Kevin held back the tears in his eyes and rolled over so he could gaze into the Jock's robin egg blue eyes. A large hand brushed through his golden locks and cradled the back of his head. Tyler's eyes were drinking him in.

"Are you okay?" Tyler asked him. Half of his handsome face lit, the other in dark shadows.

Kevin nodded his head. It was a lie. He wasn't okay. Just by being here, he could end everything. He could end his mother. He could end Tyler… He could end this beautiful heart that had earned his forgiveness. He could see his own violet eyes glowing back at him from Tyler's dark pupils.

"Thank you for staying with me," he whispered.

Tyler pulled him closer and gently squeezed. He smiled against the jock's broad chest. He was going to do everything in his power to protect those he loved. Looking up into Tyler's eyes once more, the athlete moved in closer and kissed him full on the lips. The air was charged with their mutual desire. Thunder boomed over their heads as the wind picked up. The bedroom vibrated from it, and Kevin allowed Tyler's lips to drink from him as if he were a holy well filled with living water.

CHAPTER 43

Three weeks had passed in serene silence, without a single trace or glimpse of Michael. Even little old ladies with garden hoses had ceased reporting any werewolf sightings. His home had transformed into a divine sanctuary.

The atmosphere exuded tranquillity, accompanied by a delicate and captivating fragrance that enveloped every room. The interior seemed to radiate with an ethereal glow, while the garden at the rear, where the pool lay, thrived with newfound vitality that surpassed any previous years.

Remarkably, the pool maintained its pristine condition without the need for chemical treatments. The water remained pure and refreshingly clear.

An abundance of birds, butterflies, and honeybees now graced the surroundings. The flowers bloomed with enhanced vibrancy, their beauty more captivating and their scent sweeter than ever before. Not a single biting creature could be found. Kevin found himself unable to fend off the honeybees that swarmed around him, drawn to his presence as if enchanted by his very being.

"They know a true queen when they see one," Tyler had said, making his very first out of the closet gay joke that had him laughing instead of hurting his feelings.

Officer Davidson had come by the house with her partner with zero leads as to where Michael was. There were no photos, no videos, and no fingerprints. It was like Michael had never existed. Which, in the human world, he didn't.

All the workers at the multiplex had given the very same description, which served to back Kevin up. The destruction of Cinema Room 3 was questioned, and Kevin remained silent on that matter. The security camera had not been operational that night, much to Mrs Davenport's relief.

The sketch artist's interpretation did Michael no justice. The guy couldn't get the vampire's cheekbones or eyes to look right. Michael's beauty and his horror was something that would never be captured.

Mrs Davenport had alerted him that most myths about vampires were indeed true. There would be no physical evidence of Michael's existence. A vampire cast no image and left no fingerprints.

He had always been a quick learner and he never made the same mistake twice. Daily meditations and chanting mantras helped him to learn control when he felt like screaming. Electronic devices around him tended to sizzle, spark, and explode when he got a level above annoyed.

Mrs Davenport had given him a charm that had to be empowered every day to keep him cloaked from more sensitive folks. He was reminded there were those out there who would be threatened by his mere existence.

A God on earth who was not a representative of the major faiths. The major faiths would seek to imprison him, and the pagan faiths would weaponize him.

"I wouldn't."

"You would."

"I wouldn't."

"If they took your mother or Tyler prisoner, you would do whatever they told you to do."

He opened his mouth to counter but found he could not argue with her. He loved his mother.

His feelings for Tyler had grown deeper. No one would take him from him, unless it was by the jock's choice. They were his anchors.

Staying in control was hard on even the best of days.
When he had stubbed his toe just last week, the sky had darkened, and lightning struck the road in front of his house. Crazy bursts of strength had him ripping off doors. He even ripped off Tyler's re-review mirror when he'd simply went to adjust it when the jock had finally agreed to teach him how to drive a stick.

"Genevieve!" Tyler had cried, petting the spot where the mirror had only just been and cooing against the dashboard. "He didn't mean it. Tell Genevieve you're sorry, Kevin!"

And even weirder things had started happening with Tyler as well. He was now able to lift the backend of a hummer over his head. Tyler had done that just to impress him. He had Kevin to time him, and he'd run 100 meters in 4.32 seconds. He'd picked Kevin up in his arms mermaid princess style and ran with him in 4.36 seconds. The guy didn't even break a sweat.

Tyler had also started eating like a horse. Lots of protein in his diet. His steaks got rarer and rarer.

Summer vacation had changed both their lives forever. It was clear to them that nothing was ever going to be the same for them ever again. One night, his mother had disclosed to him that his father had been the incarnation of the God Anu, the supreme Lord of Mesopotamia. Alexander Rose was the divine personification of the sky and King of the Gods.

Kevin had a stone replica made of his father's main cult image that would have been honoured all those millennia ago. A horned crown on a pedestal.

Tyler had found a cedarwood chest when they had been out antiquing, and they had both set it up as an altar in the corner of Kevin's bedroom. Kevin placed the stone relic in the centre with the photo of his dad in its silver frame in front of it. Before the photo of his dad, he put a candle and the incense burner his father had bought him in Crete with crystals all around.

Standing back, he had smiled as Tyler wrapped his arms around him and rested his chin on top of his head.

"I like it," the jock said.

Kevin grinned. "Me too."

"Should I construct and dedicate one in your honour in my bedroom?" Tyler asked him. "Candles, crystals, flowers, a lapis bowl to drip a few drops of my blood before an image of you?"

Kevin snorted.

"What about Christ? Do you think he might get upset with you?" Kevin asked. "I'm real. He could also be real."

Tyler squeezed him a little tighter and nuzzled the top of his head with his chin. "Jesus knows he will always have a seat at my table."

Kevin slowly turned around and gazed up at him with his glowing violet eyes. "Why worship a photo when I'm right here in front of you?"

The jock planted a long kiss between his brows. "I'll do anything to keep you here. I honestly think my soul belongs to you now anyway."

Little bells jingled in Kevin's ears, and he knew Tyler's words to be true. They spent the night exploring each other's bodies amidst the soft glow of candles. Light touches. Gentle caresses. Deep kisses. Nervous. Awkward. Innocence.

"Be my boyfriend?" Tyler asked, a whisper against his heart.

Kevin grinned up into his eyes. "Yes."

Tyler held him close and gently moved. Kevin's radiance filled the bedroom. Two young teenagers on the threshold of manhood allowing their souls to merge and giving love permission to blossom in their hearts.

CHAPTER 44

Two young men found solace in each other's company as they sat on a secluded stretch of Blue Grotto beach known as Siren Cove. Nestled beneath a towering bluff, they patiently awaited the sunset and the rising of a supermoon.

They had gathered driftwood and fashioned it into a roaring fire. As twilight engulfed their surroundings, mesmerizing hues of blue and lavender flickered and swirled, casting an ethereal glow before them.

Kevin stole a quick glance at Tyler and a warm smile adorned his face. The athlete reciprocated the expression, though a mixture of nervousness and excitement danced across his features.

"Tyler?" Kevin cocked his head to the side. "Is there something you want to ask me?"

The taller teen looked at him with warm blue eyes and nodded his head. Kevin held his hand.

"Are you going to Mainland?" he asked.

Kevin nodded his head. "Yes. I accepted their offer."

"That's good," Tyler said, giving his smaller hand a gentle squeeze. "I can keep a better eye on my boyfriend then."

Kevin smiled ear to ear. He loved hearing that word. Boyfriend.

"You know something," Tyler said, pulling out his new iPhone with his cordless earbuds. "I really wanted to dance with you at prom." He pulled Kevin up to his feet. "But I…"

Kevin's attention was drawn to the remarkable transformation unfolding before his eyes. He couldn't help but notice Tyler's fingers stretching and elongating, while his nails took on a newfound sharpness. As Kevin looked up into Tyler's face, he was astounded to see his features undergoing a striking metamorphosis. The jock's ears were gradually tapering into distinctive points, accentuating prominent brow bones. But the most astonishing change was yet to come. A luxuriant growth of dense, golden hair began to unfurl, covering Tyler's cheekbones and cascading down to his very chin.

"It doesn't even hurt," Tyler said, his gaze fixated on his hands. Gradually, right before their eyes, the tops of his hands sprouted a dense growth of vibrant yellow hair, while his nails elongated into sharp points. Soon enough, his muscular arms and legs were enveloped in a lustrous coat of golden fur. Even the tops of his tanned feet succumbed to this transformation, as hair began to sprout, and his toenails sharpened. "I always thought there would be pain and screams just like in the movies."

Kevin gazed deeply into Tyler's captivating blue eyes, transfixed as they gradually transformed into a mesmerizing shade of lemony orange. With a gentle touch, he placed his radiant hand against Tyler's fuzzy cheek, tenderly cradling his scruffy yet undeniably handsome face. As the magical connection intensified, Kevin's heart raced with anticipation. And then, in a startling revelation, Tyler parted his lips, unveiling a set of sharp teeth resembling those of a wolf.

"It's because I don't want you to be in pain," Kevin said to him, standing on tiptoe and kissing those brutal lips and slowly pulled away. "I make what was intended to be a curse now a blessing for all time."

The air around them shimmered and hummed with his words.

"You are mine," Kevin whispered. "For as long as you choose to be."

"I am yours." The jock smiled, revealing his sharp canines, and eagerly returned the kiss, enveloping Kevin in his muscular arms. As Tyler held him, the smaller blond could sense the careful restraint required to protect him from his mouthful of sharp teeth. In those powerful arms, Kevin radiated a mesmerizing glow, as if he were an iridescent star made flesh.

"Tyler," Kevin whispered against his chest, grinning against his warm fragrant fur. "Thank you."

The taller teen smiled and gently held the smaller blond back and Kevin gazed up into those jack-o'-lantern eyes. "I got you something for your birthday."

"You did?" Kevin asked, cocking his head to the side.

Kevin watched him turn around and kneel before the large bag beside their extra pile of driftwood. Tyler was being very mindful of his claws as he unzipped the bag, reached inside, and pulled out a rather large circular box. Kevin leaned over a broad shoulder. The jock opened the prismatic box and pulled out what was a crown of ivy vines. It was made of white jasmine flowers and the reddest roses he'd ever seen. Tyler rose back to his feet and turned to him.

Kevin eyed the delicate blossoms, lowering his head and Tyler placed it. A perfect fit. Offering accepted. Those white and red petals began to softly glow and release their scent. A halo of heavenly perfume around his head. The taller teen smiled as he then placed an earbud in his ear and carefully placed the other in Kevin's.

"To the future," Tyler said, kissing him again, staring into fathomless amethyst gems that glowed like an entire universe within that heaven filled skull.

Shimmering stardust tears came to Kevin's eyes as he gazed into Tyler's. "No matter what happens."

They both kissed again as lightning struck the rolling waves in the far distance. A sweet breeze ruffled their hair.

"Let's go to Sedona and dance in a vortex," Tyler whispered against an opaline cheek, planting soft kisses.

Kevin agreed.

Underneath the enchanting silver light of a resplendent

supermoon, a werewolf and his deity swayed gracefully in each other's arms upon the sandy shores. They danced passionately, their movements harmonizing perfectly to the haunting melody of Siouxsie and The Banshees' "The Last Beat of My Heart."

This is not the end for the future is limitless.

ACKNOWLEDGEMENTS

I want to scream a big 'THANK YOU' to my publisher, Crystal Leonardi. You have helped me make one of my dreams come true and I am so thankful.

I want to thank my amazing co-workers Elenore and Amy for taking the time to read my manuscript. Both of you gave me amazing feedback and built my confidence. It means so much to me.

Thank you, Dion Marc, for the amazing cover. Your artistic talents span dimensions. Years ago, when I first started writing this story, this is how I envisioned the characters looking. You magically pulled Kevin and Tyler from my imagination and made them manifest right before my eyes. You truly have a gift and thank you for sharing it with me.

Helen. Remember how we still laugh? *"Mama! There is a man at the door."* I love you all the way to the Hanging Gardens of Babylon and back!

And Boo. Thank you for allowing me to steal your office space after work in order to write. I love you very much!

FROM THE PUBLISHER

JB Thomas seamlessly combines contemporary romance with fantasy in his debut novel, 'Rose Red.' By blurring the edges where magic contains truth and the world as it appears is false, 'Rose Red' draws you into the lives of three very different characters; Kevin, Tyler, and Michael. Their twisted love triangle makes for a romantic thriller that proves that just about anything can happen.

The unexpected ending is a fitting denouement to an epic and memorable trip through tainted teenage love and fantasy.

It has been a great honour to work with JB Thomas for the publication of his first book, 'Rose Red.' I wish him every success and look forward to the sequel of this incredible book.

Crystal Leonardi
Bowerbird Publishing
www.crystalleonardi.com

Manufactured by Amazon.com.au
Sydney, New South Wales, Australia